BOOKS BY QUINN AVERY
www.QuinnAvery.com

BEXLEY SQUIRES MYSTERY SERIES

The Dead Girl's Stilettos

The Million Dollar Collar

The Guard's Last Watch

The Skeleton Key's Secrets

The Notebook's Hidden Truths

The Neighbor's Dark Past

STANDALONE ROMANTIC SUSPENSE/THRILLERS

What They Never Said

In Her Father's Shadow

Woman Over the Edge

Deadly Paradise

Lost Girls of Kato

Moscow Mules & Murder

Right Across the Bay

CHILDREN'S BOOKS WRITTEN BY QUINN

Dogs Don't Have Fins

Dogs Don't Have Antlers

BEXLEY
SQUIRES

THE
NEIGHBOR'S
DARK
PAST

A BEXLEY SQUIRES MYSTERY

QUINN AVERY

The Neighbor's Dark Past
Bexley Squires Mystery #6
1st Edition
Copyright © 2024 Jennifer Naumann
Cover: Najla Qamber Designs
ISBN: 979-8-9895552-9-1
Library of Congress Control Number: (applied)
www.QuinnAvery.com

PROLOGUE
PAPAYA SPRINGS, CALIFORNIA

APRIL 5TH

The man watched with rapt attention as the blonde woman bent over the flower bed, gingerly inspecting the intricate dahlia petals with the care of a mother tending to her newborn. His heart thudded with an excited staccato when his eyes feasted on her graceful hips and long, sinewy legs. Hair the color of dried wheat grass curtained her face, elbow-length and almost entirely straight with the slightest of waves at the tips.

She was nearly as beautiful as the love of his life had once been when he was a much younger man. His aging mind struggled to remember the details of her, but they shimmered at the edges with fading recollection. She'd been bold and carefree, unafraid to stand up for what she believed was right and unwilling to take direction from others. She had a light, tinkling laugh that had never failed to make him smile. Her skin was as soft and sensual as a rose petal.

They'd been in love for the better part of a year. After a few weeks, they'd begun living together in a small, rundown apartment a few blocks from the beach. She had somehow managed to transform the drab space into a welcome home with her ability to sew and make secondhand items appear new. They'd spent many late nights planning for their future together and even discussed possibly having children.

Then, one day, he had planned to surprise her with a special night, only to discover she was ending their relationship. She wasn't the slightest bit apologetic when she announced that she was leaving to explore the world on her own. He begged her to stay, or at the very least to let him join her, but she insisted she had to do it alone. He never heard from her again.

It happened long before the internet was inside every home in America, before everyone shared their every move on social media. He spent years trying to track her down before he was driven mad with agony. Before long, he began mistaking her for the woman at the bank, the woman he passed on the street, and the woman who took his order at the drive-in. He built a shrine with her pictures and various things she'd left behind and prayed to it every day that she'd return to him.

Then, one afternoon, a beautiful blonde knocked on his door, asking him if he wanted to know more about the good word of Jesus. In his desperation, he was convinced it was his love returning to him. He invited the woman inside, discreetly locking the door behind them. He only vaguely listened to her rambling about religion as he sipped a cup of lukewarm coffee. When she finished her spiel, he told her he was glad she'd returned to him. The woman's eyes had become wild, and she'd attempted to leave. He did everything he could to stop her, begging her over and over to tell the truth and to quit lying to him and herself. The next thing he knew, his hands were around her neck. Before long, the light left her eyes.

He buried her beneath the garden his One True Love had once tended that had tragically become nothing more than a dry patch of dirt and weeds.

No thanks to an old war injury, he couldn't maintain steady employment. At least it gave him the freedom to move around the country. He was desperate to find a trace of the *real* her in every city he visited, every art gallery he stepped into. There were more instances where he had similar experiences with women he believed to have been his One True Love in disguise. But none of them ended up being her.

With time, his frustration grew.

He became impatient.

He supposed he should've considered himself lucky that he had gotten by without ever making it onto law enforcement's radar, having avoided so much as a speeding ticket in decades. But ever since he'd learned the unmistakable location of his One True Love, the urge to experience the power again had kept him awake at night for months on end. He couldn't decide if the dark sensation festering in his gut that prevented him from eating or thinking straight was a deep-set anger because she had left him or if it was a need to be reunited with the only woman who'd ever had his heart.

As he watched the beautiful woman tend to her garden, it almost seemed a waste knowing what he had planned. Although he admittedly felt rusty, a thrill overpowered his nerves. It had been far too long since he'd taken a woman's life in his hands, and he was so close to being reunited with his One True Love that it was imperative he not make any mistakes.

"Best to get it out of my system before I see her," he muttered. "Then I'll be able to think clearly."

With the high pitch of the young woman's laughter, he froze. Had she heard him? Did she know he was watching and was laughing at his inept abilities? His hands balled into fists at his sides, tight enough that his fingernails drew blood.

He'd show her——

"I knew you'd call as soon as you got my message!" the woman said, rising to her feet and peeling her garden gloves from her fingers.

It was then that he noticed the white earbuds jammed inside her ears.

"Damn technology," he snarled. He couldn't take her while she was on the phone. He waited until the woman had retreated inside the house before he made his move. Ending the woman's life was only a temporary fix.

There was only one woman who could scratch the several-decades-long itch.

The sun had just crested over the hills when Currie County Sheriff's Department and detectives from the Papaya Springs precinct swarmed Anita Taylor's property. Some took pictures of the crime scene, while others secured the area with yellow tape. Several deputies spanned out to interview the gawking neighbors who had gathered with the first sound of approaching sirens.

Anita's younger sister had called 9-1-1 after discovering her older sister unresponsive on the kitchen floor. It was quickly decided by the county coroner on the scene that the cause of death had most likely been strangulation.

Deputy Danks was the one to discover a hand-written note tucked inside the victim's jeans pocket after giving her a gentle pat-down. The young deputy had initially come to California with the aspiration of becoming an actor but had decided he wanted to serve the public after portraying an officer in a movie. He'd been consuming an excessive amount of true crime documentaries for years, deciding it was more training than he would get on the job under his current employ. He remembered the story of a killer who left notes to his victims as his calling card, tucking the pieces of paper beneath his victims' bra straps.

Frowning at the strange clue, he gripped it with one gloved hand and brought it to his supervisor, Sheriff Blair.

"Found this on the victim," Deputy Danks announced, handing the note over. He felt a spurt of pride for having discovered the evidence after the detectives from the police department had examined the scene. The other deputies often teased him as he was still the department's newest hire, but he sometimes sensed they were simply jealous of his intelligence.

The sheriff smoothed a finger and thumb over his dark mustache as his beady eyes scanned the note. "*Your next, My Little Mouse,*" he read. Scoffing, he turned to Deputy Danks. "What the hell is that supposed to mean?"

"I think it means the killer intends to murder more than just this one woman, Sir." Knowing someone had died and more were likely to follow in her footsteps, Deputy Danks tried to dampen his excitement. "Seems we could potentially have another serial killer on the loose."

The sheriff scoffed and shoved the note back at his deputy. "You're getting ahead of yourself,

Danks. This might be some kind of sick foreplay from her lover."

When the sheriff shuffled away, Deputy Danks stared down at the crude scrawling on the note while fisting his other hand at his side. The sheriff may not have been willing to entertain his theory, but there was someone who certainly would… someone much more intelligent than the corrupt sheriff who only seemed interested in cases involving large sums of cash or prominent community members.

He had become friends with the woman after they'd worked on several cases together. He admired her spirit and her ability to solve complicated cases. She was part of the reason he wanted to become a detective one day.

If anyone would understand the importance of the note, it would be Bexley Squires.

PART I

CHAPTER ONE

PAPAYA SPRINGS, CALIFORNIA

APRIL 6TH

Bexley Squires crossed her arms and leaned back in her office chair, gaze honed on the blinking cursor on her computer monitor. She'd completed the online application and entered the credit card information required to process the fee but couldn't muster the courage to press RETURN on the keyboard. Wondering what could possibly be holding her back, Bexley glanced at the framed picture on her desk of herself posing with her ridiculously handsome husband just hours after he'd been released from serving time in the Papaya Springs jail. Mere minutes before they'd snapped the selfie, she'd asked him if he wanted to get married. She nearly rolled her eyes at her flushed cheeks and cheesy smile, deciding she *looked* like someone madly and ridiculously in love. The same could've been said for Brewer as he was kissing her cheek in the picture with his eyes closed and cheeks stretched to their limit with a massive smile.

While she'd learned the definition of domestic bliss since marrying Brewer Hawkins and couldn't remember a single moment in which she'd regretted the decision to elope with him, something was unnerving about officially changing her last name that she had yet to come to terms with. In truth, she lost the claim to "Squires" the moment she married another man. Still, she'd become well-respected in the community of private investigators, so a part of her was allowed to worry the change would make it harder for someone needing her services to track her down. Although Brewer hadn't pressured her in any way whatsoever to make the change, she suspected a part of her was still harboring guilt because she wasn't interested in carrying on the Hawkins surname with any rug rats. Luckily, Brewer felt the same about children.

Just as her phone dinged with a notification of local news reporting a woman had been murdered in Papaya Springs the night before, the office phone trilled with a call from a 212 number—someone in New York. It was early enough that Red, her sometimes-secretary-sometimes-tech-guru, wasn't yet in for the day, so Bexley answered on the second ring. "Stronghold Investigations, Bexley Squires speaking."

"As in Bexley *Ferguson*?" a man's deep voice inquired, sounding slightly amused.

The mention of her maiden name still managed to stir up a barrage of mixed feelings. She didn't suppose she'd ever rid herself of it. Clearing her throat, she sat a little taller. "If you want to be technical, it's Bexley *Hawkins* now." While it wasn't legally correct—at least until she hit that RETURN button—she hoped to acclimate herself to the change before making it official. It almost felt invigorating when rolling across her tongue. "How can I help you, Mr.—?"

"The website says you're going by Squires."

Bexley paused, thinking the man's voice was starting to sound familiar. "It's the twenty-first century. A woman is allowed to ponder a name change after being joined in matrimony."

The man responded with a skeptical hum. "Hopefully, this one has no falsified issues that could lead to an annulment and a deflated ego."

Her heart plummeted, making her breathless. She'd asked her first husband—something she'd agreed to on a whim as a precarious college student—to claim he couldn't sexually perform so their marriage would be wiped from all records. Her mind scrambled to recall how long it had been since she'd last spoken with the man who'd saved her from bearing her father's name any longer. When they'd been classmates at NYU, Jack Squires had been a kind and honorable man who tended to make her laugh. She hadn't thought of him in ages and wondered if he'd changed. Ironically, he was calling the exact moment she contemplated losing his name.

"*Jack?*" she exclaimed. "Is it really you?"

He released a deep chuckle that unleashed a flood of pleasant memories. "Do you have more than one ex-husband?"

"Jack! It's been…"

"Forever. Feels like a lifetime since we were a couple of wild kids, madly in love."

A warm flush spread across her skin with the mention of "love." She'd only recently become comfortable using the term of endearment with Brewer. "How are you? Are you still in New York?" *Better yet, why was he calling?*

"Things are good. I recently relocated to San Diego after accepting a big network sports commentator position."

"Congratulations, although with a face like yours, I can't say I'm surprised. I *am* surprised that you switched coasts, however. I figured you'd die before you'd move out of the city."

"I'll always be a New Yorker at heart. And I should be congratulating *you*. I understand you've made a respectable name for yourself as a private investigator."

Bexley's thoughts flashed to a 1-star review she recently received on Yelp. A disgruntled wife who'd hired Bexley to investigate a woman stalking their family wasn't too pleased to discover her husband had impregnated said stalker. Somehow, the wife had decided Bexley was to blame for her situation. "Depends who you ask."

"Well, I'm hoping you live up to the hype because I'd like to hire you to help me resolve a sensitive situation."

"I'm listening."

"I'd rather not rehash the details over the phone. Can you meet me for a quick lunch? I'm headed to Papaya Springs Academy to shadow a potential Division One recruit for the day, so something nearby that location would be ideal."

A tangle of nerves twitched inside Bexley's stomach. Brewer wasn't generally the jealous type, but he'd become increasingly romantic and sentimental since being released from jail. How would he feel if she met in private with her ex-husband? "How long will you be in town?"

"Just until tomorrow night. I'm also planning to interview the kid's coach and parents."

"How about I bring takeout to the Academy while we go over the details? Then you can come to my place tonight for dinner. It'd allow you to meet my husband, and we could catch up in a more informal setting." Brewer had thrown a beef roast and vegetables into a crockpot that morning. At least one of them had become domesticated.

Jack let out a low hum. "You might change your mind about dinner once I've brought you up to speed."

Bexley doubted that would be true. "I'll be the judge of that."

Before she powered down her computer, she hit the "return" button, officially submitting the name application, and left her office grinning.

Bexley maneuvered through the massive Papaya Springs Academy campus until she spotted Jack sitting at a small table beneath a giant flowering tree behind the gymnasium. A strong sense of déjà vu socked her in the stomach with the sight of his perfectly styled hair and chiseled features. He'd been a lighter blond when they'd met, and he'd worn his hair longer, but not much else had changed aside from his preference for jeans and band T-shirts. Jack Squires was broad-shouldered and fit with bright blue eyes that sparkled in the California sunlight as she approached. He wore a navy blue suit that made it easy to picture him sitting behind an anchor's desk, charming all of America through a camera lens.

"Bex!" he called out, swooping her into his arms for an intimate hug and nearly crushing the bag containing their lunch.

She stiffened in his hold, robotically patting his back. Far too many memories of him as her passionate lover came rushing back with his embrace. "Good to see you too, Jack."

He released her with a deep, rolling laugh. "Sorry, I forgot you weren't one for public affection." His eyes roamed over her as he let out another chuckle. "You really haven't changed. You still look fantastic."

On closer inspection, she realized he was wearing a light foundation application. "And you look camera-ready."

"We just shot a segment with the recruit," he explained. "I sent my cameraman away for lunch so I could speak with you alone."

Bexley held up the bag from Pollo's. "I hope you still like shrimp because these tacos are to die for."

He motioned to the little table where two full water bottles sat, sweating in the spring heat. "Let's dig in. Although I want to hear every detail about this new husband of yours, there will be time for that tonight."

They settled across from each other at the table. As Bexley began removing the contents from the bag, she nearly gagged. It was odd, considering Pollo's tacos were her favorite food in the entire universe. She held a wrapped taco out to Jack. "Does this smell right to you?"

He blurted, "I'm being sued for sexual harassment."

Head tilted, Bexley met his gaze. "Sued, but not prosecuted?"

"She knows she doesn't have anything substantial enough to warrant a conviction," he confirmed with a grim nod. "The accusations didn't come until she learned I'd relocated here. Now she's asking for five million in exchange for her silence." He finally accepted the taco Bexley handed him and set it down on the table with a heavy sigh. "I interned for her back in New York. She'd only been an anchor for a few months and was a handful of years older than me. One night, she invited me out for drinks and claimed everyone from the station would be there. I found her sitting alone in a corner booth when I got there. She said everyone else had canceled." He ruffled his perfect hair with one hand and glanced away. "I can't say I'm proud of what went down that night, but we were both young and single, and she was a real stunner."

"It was consensual?"

His eyes fell back on hers. "One hundred percent. If anything, she initiated it."

"So you slept together. Is there anyone who could corroborate your side of the story?"

"I didn't tell anyone because I was afraid of losing the internship."

She nodded. "That's understandable. What happened next?"

"The next day, I pretended like nothing had happened between us. She kept flirting and was constantly trying to get me alone. She finally slipped me her number, said we needed to meet again for drinks. I texted her later that night, saying I'd made a mistake and hoped the incident wouldn't interfere with my career. After that, she started harassing me…sending suggestive texts and explicit selfies." He paused, rubbing at his forehead. "One day, when she slipped a pair of her panties into my coat pocket, I decided I'd had enough. Instead of calling her out, I walked away from the internship. She disappeared from the industry after I left, only to reappear here on the West Coast a few years back. I figured I'd never have to deal with her again. Then, a couple of days ago, a Sheriff's deputy served me with a lawsuit. She's using the text saying I'd made a mistake as ammunition, claims I threatened her if she didn't sleep with me or send me nude pictures, and claims I'd stolen the underwear."

"What's this Jezebel's name?" Bexley grumbled amidst a bite of her taco.

"Tabitha Torres."

Shrimp and coleslaw stuck in her throat. "You're joking."

Jack swiped a hand over his face, suddenly appearing 10 years older. "I wish I were."

Tossing her half-eaten taco back onto its paper wrapper, Bexley leaned back on the bench. Tabitha Torres was Papaya Spring's most beloved news anchor, having survived a hostage situation involving her crazed brother-in-law. Last Bexley had heard, Tabitha earned seven figures between the network and endorsements through various clothing labels and jewelers. The news anchor had hounded Bexley for an exclusive interview after Bexley had survived a showdown with Dean Halliwell, Hollywood's brightest star turned serial killer.

"I know…it's a lot to process." Jack uncapped his water bottle and took a long swig before crossing his arms over his chest. "I think she's embarrassed that I turned her down and doesn't want me encroaching on her new turf."

"Or maybe she's merely beating you to the punch, worried *you'll* go after *her,*" Bexley suggested.

"You think that's what this is about?" A small, tentative smile curled his smooth lips. "Does that mean you believe me?"

Uncapping her water bottle, she nodded before washing the taco down. "Are you kidding me? You're one of the good guys, Jack. It makes you an easy target for powerful women like Tabitha Torres."

His smile grew, blinding Bexley with glowing white teeth. "Does that mean you'll take the case?"

"Without question. I'll even give you the ex-husband rate. Nothing makes me more upset than a woman falsely accusing a man of something he didn't do."

Jack reached across the small table to squeeze her hand. "I don't know how to thank you, Bex. What do you need from me?"

"Bring the papers you were served to dinner." She pulled her hand away from his with a friendly smile. "And you're gonna want to change out of that suit before you come over. Our place has more of a barefoot-in-the-sand kind of vibe."

They finished their tacos in silence. Before they parted ways, Bexley gave him her home address. Although she genuinely believed Jack's side of the story, a part of her was nervous that Jack's affectionate ways would ignite a new side of Brewer she had yet to witness.

CHAPTER TWO

Moments after Bexley parked beside her husband's classic GTO in the driveway of their slice of heaven on the beach, her phone buzzed with an incoming call from their eccentric neighbor. Twila occasionally watched Brewer and Bexley's rescue dog, Captain, and had been casually dating Bexley's former boss and friend, J.J. Stronghold, for several months. She had become a surrogate mother of sorts to Bexley, constantly checking in and giving her worldly advice.

She answered with a smile that could be heard in her voice, "No, I have not tried those 'special' cookies you baked me—"

"It's not that," Twila assured her. "Hope I'm

not bothering you. I'm calling because…I believe I'm in need of your services."

Bexley slid out of the car and engaged the locks. "Have you talked to J.J. about whatever's going on? You know he's always looking for something to keep him busy."

"I will have to ask that you use discretion on this one, Bexley. J.J. mustn't know."

"I can be discreet," Bexley promised, reaching for the handle on their front door. It would be difficult to keep something from her mentor, but she'd do it for Twila. She only hoped it wasn't anything too serious. "I'm just walking into our place, Twila. Give me ten minutes, and I'll stop over."

"Thank you, my dear. I'm sure having to work after hours is the last thing you want, so I put a bottle of that sparkling wine you like on ice."

Inside, Bexley was greeted by Captain's enthusiastically warm tongue and the blast of rock music. Brewer's deep baritone from outside joined in with the singer's raspy voice on the chorus, attempting an octave too high for his range. Bexley slapped a hand over her mouth to contain a sudden burst of laughter. She couldn't believe the myriad of ways Brewer continued to surprise her in the time they'd been together.

She gave the wiggling mass of blag fur the appropriate amount of attention, scratching the dog's belly and behind his ears before she kicked off her shoes and ventured farther inside the cottage, discovering the sliding doors in the back wide open. Brewer knelt on the patio, brushing stain over the rocking horse he'd slaved over for weeks.

Bexley leaned against the open door, legs crossed at her ankles, admiring the view of her handsome husband at work with the Pacific Ocean roaring off in the distance. He still wore the same sleeveless T-shirt and old jeans he'd left in that morning for work, but his shirt was covered in dark spots of oil—*likely another one for the trash*, she noted with mild irritation. She'd been unable to talk him into wearing coveralls to save his wardrobe.

His arms weren't quite as massive as they'd been after he'd served his jail time, but they still held a respectable amount of muscular mass in proportion with the rest of his fit body. His brown hair was long enough to tuck behind his ears, and a few days' worth of scruff lined his fierce jaw. Before she'd been reunited with her old classmate while on a case, she never would've dreamed she'd fall for someone as rough around the edges or someone with more inked than untouched skin. She'd also never been with a man who'd worn his heart on his sleeve or had been so understanding of her passion.

She thought she might burst into tears when she envisioned Brewer crafting another rocking horse for *their* child. Although her too-cute-for-words nephew had wormed his way into her non-maternal heart since he came into the world three months prior, she still wasn't ready to sacrifice their flexible lifestyle to care for a baby. Whenever the subject came into conversation, Brewer agreed it wasn't something he was prepared for either—maybe ever.

She inhaled the briny air that always helped her instantly relax and beamed at her husband. "I can't decide if you're vying for the title of favorite uncle or practicing for an audition with Dave Grohl."

Brewer spun around to face her with a devilishly attractive grin, honeyed brown eyes shining brighter than the stars above them. A streak of dark stain grazed his cheek, and another ran along one of his forearms. "Welcome home, beautiful."

They embraced for a long, satisfying kiss that made her belly buzzy. She even felt a little dizzy when she backed away, still gripping his broad hips. "Now, *that* was a greeting worth coming home to. Does your enthusiasm have anything to do with the fact that you're about to meet my first husband?"

He answered the question with a lighthearted chuckle, then kissed her forehead. "Not at all. Can't a man simply be happy to see his hot wife after a long day?"

"That sentiment will never grow old," she decided, kissing the tip of his nose. "While you clean up, I'm going to run over to Twila's. She just called to say she wants to hire me for something but doesn't want J.J. to know about it."

Brewer's dimpled smile evaporated. He had become just as close with Twila as Bexley had, even once referring to her as the mother he wished he'd had. "Everything alright?"

"I don't know. Hopefully, it's nothing too serious." She began to turn away. Brewer stopped her, drawing her back into his arms. Bexley was convinced the sinful smile he gave her could literally melt butter. "Just so you know, I'm not getting in the shower until you return to join me."

"Now, *that* would be an awkward way for you to meet my ex." Laughing, she squeezed her arms around him. "Go clean up on your own, Hawk. There isn't time for those shenanigans…at least not until later tonight, after he's left."

Through the open back door of Twila's small cottage, Bexley found the home to be just as warm and welcoming as always. The gentle lull of a piano and a woman's breathy tenor played from the antique turntable in the living room. A soft, twinkling glow emanated from a lamp covered with a piece of sheer pink fabric adorned with rhinestones. The strong scent of fresh flowers and incense sparked Bexley's senses when she prepared to announce her arrival. She realized there was no need as Captain had already slipped past her, and Twila was gushing his name in greeting.

"Bexley, come on in!" Twila called from the kitchen. "Your glass is on the table!"

Bexley swiped the hand-painted glass tumbler off the table and took a long, satisfying sip of the Prosecco as she watched Twila give Captain a homemade dog treat. She couldn't help but notice her neighbor's long silver hair flowing down her slender back rather than being in its usual braid. She also wore a colorful kimono paired with whimsical, uncharacteristically wrinkled pants. The normal oodles of gypsy-like jewelry were oddly absent.

"Thanks—I needed this after the day I had,"

Bexley said. She'd spent her afternoon researching Tabitha Torres's lawsuit and had decided Jack was in for an uphill battle against the wealthy star. "What did you want to talk to me about? Is everything alright?"

Twila gestured to Captain with a hand, and he stood on his hind legs to give her a high-five. Laughing, she shook her head at Bexley. "It's nothing, really. But it seems I'm being harassed. Or… maybe even stalked."

"That's far from *nothing*, Twila." Concern weighed heavily inside Bexley's stomach. "What's going on?"

"I've received two phone calls this week that involved nothing but heavy breathing. And just yesterday, I received a strange package. Someone sent me several daffodil bulbs."

"Could you have ordered the bulbs a while back and forgot?"

Shrugging, Twila bent to scratch Captain behind an ear. "Doubtful. There wasn't an invoice, and the bulbs were simply thrown in the box without any packaging."

"What about a return address?"

"There wasn't one."

"Do you still have the box?"

"It's in the garage."

Bexley took a long swig of her drink. She was starting to understand Twila's concern. "I'd like to see it before I leave."

"There's one more thing…" Twila attempted a friendly smile, but her lips trembled, and her blue eyes sparkled with moisture. "It's better if I show you."

After Twila commanded Captain to stay, Bexley set her glass back on the table before following her to the front door facing the road. Twila opened it and stepped aside so Bexley could see the dead albino mouse on her front step.

"It was here this afternoon when I headed out to run a few errands." Twila squeezed her hands together, grimacing. "I didn't move it, so you could see exactly how I found it."

Bexley bent down to inspect the rodent and snap pictures with her cell phone. It was clearly not the type of mouse that lived in the wild. It must've been purchased from a pet store. As much as she wanted to tell Twila it was nothing to be concerned about, the way its neck hung slack in an unnatural direction from its body made it clear it had been broken. The creature's death was no accident.

"The poor little guy," Twila said, her voice thickening with unshed tears. "Who would do such a thing?"

Bexley glanced up at her. "Can you think of anyone who might be upset with you enough to do something like this?" Although the idea of anyone having a grudge against her sweet neighbor seemed ludicrous, it was the first question she asked any of her clients in similar situations.

"I no longer know very many people in Papaya Springs. Pretty much all of my friends and family in the area have either died or moved on since I lived here last."

"What about someone from your past? Someone who doesn't live in the area but may have tracked you down through your art?"

"They can do that?"

"Your work is featured on the gallery's website," Bexley reminded her, standing to touch her neighbor's arm. "Are you sure you don't want to tell J.J. what's happening? I'll keep my word and not say anything, but Twila, this could be serious business."

"You know how his health has been. I'm afraid this kind of thing could put him in the hospital."

"There isn't anyone you can think of who might be angry with you?"

Twila swiped a wayward piece of hair away from her face with a deep sigh. "I've been wracking my brain all afternoon. There was an older girl who tirelessly harassed me in middle school for having a long neck, but I found her obituary online. I honestly can't think of anyone else."

"Sounds to me like this older girl was simply jealous of your beauty." Bexley bit down on a smile, amused that Twila would think a bully from sixty-some years ago would return with a vengeance. "I'm going to dispose of this little guy before I head home with Cap and that box from the garage. Why don't you come over in half an hour and join us for dinner? Brewer can install some cameras on your property when we're done. We have some left over from a package he bought before he went to jail." Bexley could add the live feed to her phone app and keep an eye on Twila's house throughout the day.

Twila cocked her head. "I thought Brewer said you were having company over for dinner."

"As a matter of fact, we are, and I'd love to have you there as a buffer." Laughing, Bexley ushered Twila through the open door. "My new husband is about to meet my old husband."

"You mean the hottie you married in college?"

"That'd be the one. He's a sports commentator and just moved out here."

"Dinner *and* a show?" Twila's eyes sparkled with mischief. "You don't have to ask me twice."

CHAPTER THREE

Brewer emerged from their bathroom as Bexley returned home to freshen up and change. His hair was slicked back, and he wore a long-sleeved, white button-down and tan chinos that her best friend, Kiersten, had gifted him from an up-and-coming designer. Bexley sensed he was overly worried about making a good first impression.

"Damn, it Hawk, I just invited Twila to join us for dinner," Bexley teased, snaking her arms around his neck and inhaling the designer cologne she had gifted him for his birthday. "Now I'm going to have to spend the entire night making sure she doesn't steal my man. Must you look so undeniably attractive?"

Brewer's expression remained rigid as he studied his reflection over the dresser. "Does this look alright?"

She snorted. "Definitely not alright. More like *amazing*."

He ruffled his hair with an unsteady hand, giving it that attractive, messed-up-in-a-sexy-way look that male models are known for creating. "I don't know, B. Some of these clothes Kiersten likes to send—"

"Would you quit acting like a pubescent girl going to her first junior high dance and look at me?" She gripped his chin, literally forcing him to meet her gaze. "Jack's a nice guy who isn't going to judge you for whatever ridiculous reason is going through that gorgeous head of yours. I promise. Even if he wasn't, since when do you care what other people think? You're a veteran, and a successful business owner, and a kind soul, and the best husband someone like me could hope for. I'm so stinking proud of you that it's probably border-line illegal. I'm your wife; therefore, my opinion is the only one that counts. Got it?"

He blinked so hard that Bexley wondered if he was actually fighting back tears. "What if spending time with him tonight reminds you of everything you gave up when you left him? What if you have second thoughts about our arrangement and realize someone like him could give you more?"

"More what?" she challenged, clicking her tongue. "More laughter…love…happiness…heartfelt moments? More *tattoos*?" Sniggering, she moved her hand to his chest, where he'd recently covered an old tattoo with the letter "B" over his heart. "What could I *possibly* want more of that you aren't already giving me?"

"The guy signed a ten million dollar contract, B." His gaze briefly shifted away from hers. "I looked it up before I got into the shower."

Anger simmered through Bexley as she stared into the depths of his warm chestnut eyes. Maybe she had every right to be nervous about Brewer finally meeting her first husband. "After all we've been through together…do you seriously think I'd be impressed by that kind of money? Where is this insecurity coming from, Hawk? This isn't like you."

"You wouldn't have to work so hard if you were with someone like him." His Adam's Apple bobbed with a deep swallow. "Sometimes I worry what I have to offer isn't enough for someone like you."

"*Someone like me*?" she nearly choked. "We don't have time to unpack what you mean by that."

With a tight laugh, she pulled him over to sit on the edge of their bed. "Listen very carefully, Brewer Hawkins. I don't know how you came up with these ridiculous ideas, but I never cared about Jack anywhere near as much as I care for you. It was a short fling, and I can't even say I was truly in love. You and me? We have a crazy good thing going. Neither one of us is perfect, and that makes us perfect for *each other*. I've never loved any other man the way I love you, and I promise you're the only one I'll ever love that way. I wouldn't trade this life—this *home*—we have built together for anything. *Anything*, Hawk. Do you understand me?"

One side of Brewer's mouth lifted in a crooked smirk. "Even if Jack came here tonight and offered you free Pollo tacos for life?"

"Now *that* I may have to think on for an extra minute or two." With a noisy snort, she dragged him close and kissed him deeply, feeling dizzy by the time they parted. They stared into each other's eyes for a moment, foreheads still pressed together. "If I ever hear ridiculous words like that coming from your mouth again, I'm going to have a neuro-surgeon check you for brain damage." She playfully pushed him back and rolled her eyes. "I'm starting to think you hit your head a few times while patrolling the ocean for the Coast Guard."

Brewer worked on grilling the Tomahawk steak he had insisted on running out to buy after Bexley told him Jack was coming to dinner. At the exact time Bexley had told Jack to arrive, there was a knock on the front door. Twila beat Bexley to the door, swinging it open to reveal Jack wearing a black button-down and blue jeans, a bottle of Prosecco in hand. Although he was still undeniably handsome, Bexley felt nothing beyond happiness to see her old friend.

"So you're the ex-husband?" Twila challenged, hands on her hips. Cap sat obediently at the woman's side, big eyes honing in on Jack in expectation of making a new friend.

"Yes, ma'am," Jack replied with an amused smirk. He held out one hand. "You must be Bexley's sister whom I never had the pleasure of meeting."

Twila's eyes briefly swept up and down his body before she shrugged. "I suppose I can understand the attraction." Instead of shaking his hand, she snagged the bottle from his grip and returned to the kitchen. Cap gave Jack a regretful look before he trailed close behind.

Bexley slipped in next to Jack. "That's our good friend and neighbor, Twila." Holding a hand beside her mouth, she stage-whispered, "She'll warm up once she decides she likes you."

"I'll have her asking for my number before the night ends," he teased with a wink.

Laughing, Bexley motioned for him to follow her to the patio out back. "Come on, I'll introduce you to Brewer."

They found her current husband slaving over the hot grill, sleeves rolled to his elbows. He wore the "Mr. Good Lookin' is cookin'" apron gifted to him by Cineste, and his hair was even messier than before. Bexley hummed in appreciation beneath her breath, wondering how someone like Brewer could possess a single ounce of self-doubt.

"That looks amazing," Jack declared, nodding at the grill. "I've never been able to get a tomahawk cooked to that perfection. What's your secret?"

Hawk's gaze snapped over to Jack. "I'd tell you, but then I'd have to kill you."

Both men chuckled as they simultaneously stepped toward one another to shake hands.

"Brewer Hawkins. It's a pleasure to meet you, brother."

Jack's expression was nearly identical when he took Brewer's hand. "Jack Squires. And likewise. Based on what Bex told me earlier today, I'm glad to hear she's settled down with a good man like you."

Bexley secretly released the breath she'd been figuratively holding since her bazaar conversation with Brewer earlier. Fortunately, any insecurities her husband was holding onto seemed to have evaporated. And as a bonus, lightning hadn't struck anyone after their introduction.

Seeing the two men together was a wild trip she didn't think she'd ever experience. They were both undeniably handsome in their own ways. If someone had told her back when she was with Jack that it would be a tattooed, former bad boy who would forever have her heart, she would've busted a rib laughing. Grinning, she dramatically clapped her hands together. "Now that we have *that* out of the way, would either of you gentlemen like a drink? We seem to have a plethora of Prosecco on hand in addition to just about anything else your hearts may desire."

"You feel like making an old fashioned?" Brewer

asked with a lopsided grin. He turned to Jack, nudging him with an elbow. "Her smoked version is legendary at our house."

Jack nodded once, clapping his hand against Brewer's back. "How can I turn that down?"

Bexley swung her arms at her sides. "I'm on it!" She spun around and raced inside, temporarily plopping down onto one of the rustic stools at the kitchen island to catch her breath. *What had just happened?* One minute, Brewer was joking about killing Jack. The next, it was as if they were old friends.

"That seems to have gone better than you were expecting," Twila commented, eyeing the men through the kitchen window before setting a glass of Prosecco in front of Bexley. "Take a sip or two—it'll help bring you out of shock."

Once everyone was stuffed from Brewer's stellar cooking and the table was cleared, Twila sat alongside Bexley on the patio, watching Brewer and Jack take turns throwing Cap's football. Although the sun had set long ago, the moon was bright enough that the men's teeth glowed in the silvery light every time they laughed. Bexley's two husbands had bonded even more over dinner and planned to meet up for a game of pickleball the following week. She secretly wished someone would pinch her to confirm it wasn't a dream.

The only moment of discomfort came when Jack asked during their meal if Bexley planned to continue working after they started a family. Bexley had just popped a forkful of rice into her mouth and spewed it across her plate, sprinkling her meal with colorful grains. Brewer met her gaze across the table and chuckled heartily, his eyes gleaming with an equal mix of amusement and empathy.

"It's rude to assume every married couple plans to have children," Twila had chided Jack with a stern look. Bexley somehow resisted bumping knuckles with the woman and miming a mic drop.

"There are times I wish I had a husband," Twila admitted between sips of her wine. "I had my share of lovers in the past, but none made me want to settle down—at least until I met your mentor." She turned to give Bexley a sad smile. "And we both know how that will most likely end, considering J.J.'s health."

Bexley patted the back of her friend's free hand. She had invited J.J. to join them for dinner, but he wasn't having a good day when Bexley had called. Bexley feared their time with him was dwindling, so it made her insanely happy to see him living out the end of his life with the kind woman.

"He seems to come alive when you're around," she told Twila. "I'm glad the two of you found each other." She retrieved her own flute of wine and observed the men from behind the rim. "Do you think any of your past lovers would want to rattle your cage for any reason?"

"I don't see how," Twila decided with a shake of her head.

"We already talked about this, Twila. They would only have to find your website to know you're local to Papaya Springs."

The elderly woman sighed with a faraway look. "I just mean they were all good men. We parted ways on good terms."

All at once, two men paused their game and huddled together, pointing at something in the direction of Twila's house. Concern lined Brewer's face.

"Stay here for a minute," Bexley told Twila, handing her what was left of her wine. "I'll be right back."

She sprinted up to Brewer. "What's going on?"

"I saw a flashlight bouncing around Twila's yard," he told her, still frowning in that direction.

"If she's having problems with intruders, maybe we should call the police," Jack suggested.

Bexley squeezed Brewer's impressive bicep before starting to move away. "I'll check——"

"No way." Brewer tugged her back to his side. "Do you have your stun gun?"

"It's in the Expedition," she admitted sheepishly.

After releasing a deep grunt, he turned back to Jack. "Do me a solid and keep her here while *I* check it out. She refuses to carry a pistol." His somber gaze returned to Bexley. "If I'm not back in five minutes, call the police."

"Brewer——" she began to protest, but she was cut off when his lips sealed over hers.

He backed away with a soft glare. "Not up for discussion, Squires."

As he raced away, she muttered, "Actually, it's *Hawkins* now."

Jack chuckled at her side. "He doesn't know you took his name?"

"I haven't had a chance to tell him," she admitted with a stuttering breath. Her eyes tracked Brewer until he disappeared into the shadows.

"Don't suppose I could convince you to let me follow him? You could tell him I knocked you out to save your pride."

"Are you kidding me? Like you said, he's a great guy, but I wouldn't want to get on his bad side. I get the feeling he could bench me with one hand tied behind his back."

Bexley tapped her chin. "Is it wrong that I kinda want to see that scenario play out?"

In the distance, a man gave an unintelligible shout. Bexley's wide-eyed expression met Jack's for only a moment before she was in motion.

She tripped and almost fell with the unmistakable sound of gunfire.

CHAPTER FOUR

Bexley's frantic heartbeats rattled her entire body as she sprinted to Twila's property. She heard feet pounding in the sand somewhere behind her—presumably belonging to Jack—and a set of protective barks from Cap. She hoped her favorite pastime of running would give her enough of a head-start to ensure the danger would be over before they caught up to her.

"Hawk!" she whispered somewhat loudly. Part of her was afraid he wouldn't want to answer and reveal his location to the shooter. She couldn't stand to ponder the other heartbreaking reasons he might not be able to respond otherwise.

Twila's meticulously maintained clapboard house and yard remained dark beneath her vast canopy of Jacaranda trees. Bexley sprinted around the side of the property and approached the motion light illuminating the front step.

Another white mouse lay motionless beneath the door in a way that made it clear the first one hadn't been an accident.

A chill ran through Bexley as she carefully scanned the broad front yard. She acknowledged the intruder could jump out from the dense land-scaping. In any other situation, she would've retreated because of the threat and called the police. But she wasn't going anywhere until she knew whether or not her husband had been harmed.

"Hawk!" Her throat tightened around his name. "Please answer me!"

With the sound of footsteps pounding the road, she ducked behind the massive bulk of Twila's prized roses. Her heart stilled momentarily until Brewer's face appeared beneath the yardlight. He suddenly stopped, resting his hands on his knees while he caught his breath. Bexley rushed over to him.

"Are you okay?" she demanded in an unusually high voice, forcing him to stand upright so she could get a good look at all of him. "Were you shot?"

"I'm good," he promised, pulling her in for a firm, one-armed embrace before kissing her head. "Bastard squeezed off a few before I could get a good look at him. He took off running and somehow slipped into the dark before I could catch up."

"Did you see him at all?" she asked, resting her hand on his chest as she backed away. "Could you give any kind of a description?"

"Average-sized—definitely the build of a man," he panted. "Ran like one too. Beyond that…it was too dark. Sorry, B."

Jack came in behind them, his breaths spilling even heavier than Brewer's. "I called the police. Dispatch said they'll be ten to fifteen minutes out." His gaze scanned over each of them. "Everyone alright?"

"The intruder's gone," Brewer informed him, bending to pet Cap's head when their loyal pet sat at his feet. The way his ears were pinned to his head, he clearly felt their tension. "But if you don't mind sticking around a little longer, I'd like to install a few cameras around here as soon as possible and could use some help."

Jack gave a firm nod. "Count me in."

Bexley felt a rush of gratitude for her husband's determination and need to protect their friend. "I'll check on Twila, then make up the guest room," she told him. "No way she's sleeping here tonight."

Brewer tilted his chin at Jack. "You should go back with her to check on Twila. I'll wait for the police. I'm sure they'll want to talk to each of us eventually."

Feeling anxious after leaving Twila all alone—*what if the intruder had snuck over there once Brewer lost him?*—Bexley sprinted back to their cottage. Relief washed over her when she found Twila sitting in the same spot she'd left her, blissfully seeming unaware of the situation the way she sipped her wine. Cap barked a friendly greeting from behind Bexley before nuzzling up to the older woman.

"What's going on?" Twila demanded, sinking her hands into Cap's fur. "Why are you out of breath?"

"Everything's going to be okay," Bexley assured her with a gentle smile. She was torn about revealing too much, afraid of frightening the old woman. But since a deadly weapon had been discharged, Bexley assumed the visitor had nothing but nefarious intentions. "There was an intruder at your house. Brewer got it under control and the police are on their way. You're staying here with us tonight."

"The police?" Twila shot to her feet. "Where's Brewer? Is he alright?"

"He's fine. He's waiting to speak with the officers. They'll probably want to ask you some questions, too." Bexley lowered to her neighbor's side. "There was another white mouse on your doorstep, Twila. I need you to think hard about what kind of message this intruder might be trying to give you. Did you ever have a specific involvement with mice? Maybe you painted one at some point or had one as a pet?"

For the first time since they'd met Twila Finn, the woman appeared closer to eighty than Bexley realized. Her wrinkles deepened as she stroked her fingers over her forehead. "I can't…I mean, I don't remember anything off the top of my head. I guess I've always loved animals." Her watery eyes met Bexley's. "Do you suppose that could be the connection?"

As Jack jogged up to the patio, Bexley gave him a weary look. "I'm not sure," she answered, rubbing a hand against Twila's back. "Whoever it may be,

I'm going to try my hardest to stop them before they get to you."

Bexley acknowledged it was a bold declaration, considering she didn't have a single lead.

Bexley arrived at the office the following morning with a massive wave of exhaustion riding on her shoulders. After receiving Jack's call, Sheriff Blair had taken nearly forty-five minutes to arrive. Once he realized Brewer and Bexley were involved, he seemed to lose any interest in the case. He had only "investigated" for maybe twenty minutes before declaring it was probably a homeless person or a tweaker looking for a fix. It was as if he hadn't heard Brewer mention there had been a gun involved.

Brewer and Jack had worked on installing the cameras beneath the intense power of shop lights from their garage. Bexley and Twila had gone to sleep in their respective beds hours before the men returned. Brewer kissed Bexley when he crawled into bed, letting her know everything was taken care of and that he had insisted Jack crash for the night on their couch.

An intense sensation had come over her when she looked into her husband's dark eyes, glistening in the moonlight streaming through their window. She wasn't sure if it was because she'd feared for his life earlier, she still hated the way he'd expressed his fear of not being enough for her, or because she was suddenly reminded of his brave nature. Most likely, it was a combination of the three. Whatever it was, she felt an overwhelming need to remind him of how much he was loved. They had spent the next several hours getting lost in each other.

Cheeks warm with the memory, Bexley's lips spread with a broad smile as she pushed open the front door of Stronghold Investigations. The elevated mood evaporated when she spotted Tabitha Torres waiting beside the receptionist's desk.

The celebrity anchor wore a black sports coat over a black bodysuit, and black heels. Her shoulder-length, jet-black hair was curled and styled in camera-ready perfection. Her olive complexion was flawlessly smooth, accentuated by plump lips coated in a velvety shade of red. She was a natural beauty by anyone's standards and possessed a vibe that commanded respect.

Bexley had no intention of giving it to her.

"Bexley Squires…we finally meet," Tabitha stated, her expressively wide, dark eyes honing in on Bexley the same way Cap fixated on a juicy bone. Although the woman's voice was high and brisk, it still omitted sex appeal. Bexley had followed Tabitha's career long enough to know the woman had clawed her way to becoming the network's prized anchor. She was attractive, and the general public trusted her to report the truth. *If they only knew,* Bexley mused.

"That's right," Bexley confirmed, careful to bite back on the sarcastic replies festering in the depths of her mind. She quickly decided that knocking the celebrity off her pedestal was the best route. "And you are…?"

"Tabitha Torres."

Behind the desk, Red sprang to her feet like a broken Jack in the Box. Her somber expression starkly contrasted her ultraviolet dress, colorful Star Wars tattoos, and retro bouffant hairdo. "Ms. Torres is here to see you."

Bexley gave a curt nod. "I'll be with you in a moment, Ms. Torres," she announced with a stiff smile, veering toward her office. She closed the door, leaning against it while catching her breath and willing her heart to stop hammering. She promised herself she wouldn't be intimidated by the powerful woman, nor would she appear to be anything short of professional. With the *ding* of an incoming message on her computer, she scurried over to her desk.

Want me to tell her you have an emergency to tend to? Red had typed. *She seems…agitated.*

I can hold my own with her, Bexley typed in reply.

I have zero doubts about that, Red responded. *Just offering to save you a headache.*

Give me five minutes before bringing her in. Then start digging into everything you can find on the woman.

10-4, bosslady.

Bexley admitted she was stalling when she scrolled through her emails and fingered the stack of phys-ical mail before checking on the video app to ensure Twila's cameras were in proper working order. She was only nervous because the news anchor was skilled at twisting the truth and making it believable.

A few minutes later, when a light knock on her door rang out, Bexley sat rigidly behind her desk.

She braced herself as Red opened the door to usher the woman inside.

Tabitha strode into the room with the aura of a superstar. A trail of expensive perfume and hair products followed her inside. Bexley at least admired the woman's confidence, even though she falsely accused Jack of something heinous.

"Thank you, Red," Bexley called out before the door was closed.

Tabitha eyed the chair facing Bexley, then defiantly lifted her sculpted chin. She clearly wasn't going to lower herself to Bexley's level, figuratively or literally. "I don't believe in wasting time with small talk, so I'll make this painless for the both of us. My attorneys tell me you contacted them with questions about my lawsuit against Jack Squires."

Bexley leaned back, crossing her arms over her stomach. "I have a copy of the complaint in my possession. I wanted to gauge for myself whether or not they had anything concrete to support the claim."

The woman's excellently sculpted eyebrows rose. "And what exactly did you conclude?"

"That your lawsuit is frivolous."

"That's odd," Tabitha bit out. "Like you, I also

studied journalism at NYU. Somehow, my degree didn't make *me* an expert in matters of the law."

Bexley lifted one shoulder, unbothered. "I don't need a law degree to know Jack is innocent."

Tabitha released a dry, bitter laugh. "What exactly is your interest in the matter, *Miss Squires*? I assume you're somehow related to Jack?"

"Matter of fact, I'm his ex-wife. Our marriage was short-lived, but we've remained good friends."

Setting a slender hand on her hip, Tabitha's red lips puckered with a sneer. "That would explain your loyalty to him. I imagine any female who has slept with him has likely fallen under the same spell, considering his 'talents' in the bedroom. Fortunately, I was strong enough to see through his act for what it was."

"And what was that, exactly?"

"He *preys* on successful women."

It was Bexley's turn to sneer. "Jack's no predator. And he never had me under any kind of *spell*. Say one more derogatory thing, and he'll be countersuing you for libel." Bexley set her elbows on her desk and laced her fingers together. "Don't assume my relationship with him affects my ability to expose this lawsuit for what it really is, Ms. Torres."

"And what might that be?"

"I haven't decided yet. Resentment? Regret? Jealously?" She sat back in her chair, studying Tabitha's bitter scowl. "Let's be honest—we both know you were the aggressor in the encounter between you and Jack. What reason would you possibly have to pursue this lawsuit nearly a decade after the harassment *allegedly* occurred?"

"Let me give you a little friendly advice, Miss Squires. Woman to woman." Tabitha moved in closer, setting a hand on Bexley's desk as she leaned in. Up close, the glare of her unnaturally white teeth was almost blinding. "I've spent many years in journalism, and I can tell you one absolute truth about human nature: people aren't always what they seem, and their intentions are rarely good." Her dark eyes radiated a simmering rage, sending a chill through Bexley. "Drop your little investigation before someone *accidentally* gets hurt."

Once the threat was delivered, Tabitha spun around and marched out the door.

Bexley was convinced more than before that Tabitha possessed a secret motive behind the lawsuit. She couldn't wait to expose it.

CHAPTER FIVE

Tabitha Torres had only been out of Stronghold Investigations for a few minutes before Red breezed into Bexley's office. "It probably won't come as a surprise that the woman doesn't have much to hide. Aside from being held hostage by a brother-in-law who had snapped with no real explanation even after his trial, her background is clear. The only dirt I could find involved a little spat with a classmate who'd won the homecoming queen label Tabitha had been vying for and something fishy about a grade she received in tenth-grade geometry."

Bexley blinked several times. "I don't pay you *nearly* enough."

"She lives alone in a five-bedroom mansion

near Highland Park," Red continued, handing over a small stack of papers. "She purchased her home in twenty-twenty and paid the mortgage off in under a year. No marriages, no children, and no current romantic relationships that I could find. Her parents each died before she graduated high school. The only family she has left involves a sister and a young nephew. Her online portfolio claims she's involved with a few local charities, but she's not listed on any boards." She paused, fingering the collection of earrings in her right ear. "Sorry, I don't have anything juicy to tell you. Going off her online presence, she's squeaky clean. But I'd bet my Mandalorian helmet prop replica she's hiding a pile of dirt. No one can live up to the level of perfection she portrays."

"I guess that was to be expected." Bexley sat back in her comfortable office chair, contemplating closing her eyes and taking a quick nap. "Compile a list of her coworkers and any friends or family you can find and include their contact info. I doubt any of them will be willing to talk with me, but it might be our only avenue for now. That and a little old-fashioned spying."

Red stared at her for a moment. "You look a little…err…peaked. Everything alright?"

"It was a late night. Brewer had a close run-in with an intruder at our neighbor's house, and we hosted company overnight. After you're done with this Tabitha Torres mess, do me a favor and look into anything you can find about mice in modern and past cultures."

The level of exhaustion running through her was unlike anything she'd felt before. She decided it would take an entire six-pack of her favorite pineapple-flavored Mexican soda from Pollo's to get her through the day. But then she remembered the off smell of the tacos she'd shared with Jack, and once again, her stomach sloshed with unease.

"When you're done with those things, you can check out for the weekend. Kiersten wants me to meet her for a late lunch and arrange things for the party tomorrow. After that, I'll probably call it a day."

Red's emerald eyes narrowed. "Ooo, I almost forgot about the adoption party! Have you seen your costume yet?"

"No," Bexley muttered, finally closing her eyes. "And I don't want to talk about it."

Temperance Rose had insisted on throwing a massive party once her daughter Olive's adoption was official. The mother-daughter duo decided the party would double as a benefit for local animal shelters. To Bexley's dismay, they had chosen a Medieval theme that stemmed from Olive's love of fairytales involving princesses and queens and insisted anyone in attendance dress accordingly.

Of course, Kiersten had jumped at yet another opportunity to style Bexley as if she were a living doll. Bexley couldn't imagine what crazy getup her friend was making her wear this time.

Early on Saturday morning, as Brewer and Cap continued to sleep soundly in their bed, Bexley skipped her usual morning run to check on Twila. Since their neighbor had insisted on sleeping at her house the night before, Bexley had been awake for over half the night, checking the app for any activity or malfunction. As a result, she wasn't sure how she would keep her head from dropping into a bowl of punch at Temperance's party.

Although Twila was still dressed in her satin pajamas beneath a rose-printed robe and appeared bleary-eyed, she had pineapple mimosas ready for Bexley's arrival. As she handed one of the drinks to Bexley, the all-knowing woman shook her head at the sight of the bags underneath Bexley's eyes.

"You clearly spent the entire night worrying about me. I should've stayed with you again."

After taking a sip of her drink, Bexley shrugged one shoulder. "The cameras are doing their job. I'm sure tonight will be better." She tilted her head at Twila. "Have you had a chance to consider anyone for a list of suspects? Anyone at all?"

"I started looking through my photo albums last night. Like I said, everyone I've dated or befriended in my lifetime had gentle spirits."

"That's probably because you're more trusting than most," Bexley scolded. "If you don't have anything better to do today, maybe you could come up with a list of the people from those albums along with whatever details you can remember—how you met, where they lived, and any other helpful information you can give me."

"I'm an old woman," Twila pondered. "That list could take me months."

"We don't have the luxury of time, and I need to start *somewhere*, Twila." She felt guilty for playing dirty when she added, "Don't make me bring J.J. into this."

"Fine," Twila relented, eyes narrowed. "I'll make the damn list."

———

Bexley returned home an hour later to prepare for the party. When Kiersten revealed the costumes after lunch the day before, Bexley didn't necessarily *hate* the leather-clad corset and full skirt paired with a quiver of rubber arrows. The look made her feel pretty badass. And it had been easy enough to style her hair in simple braids like Kiersten suggested.

However, there were no words for how she felt about the pirate-style vest over a black blouse and pants that Kiersten had tailor-made by a celebrity designer for Brewer. When he stepped out of the bathroom moments before they left, Bexley wasn't sure how she mustered the willpower not to strip him down or, at the very least, make him dance. She couldn't stop staring as they piled into her husband's GTO with Olive's presents and Cap—who wore a green Robin Hood-style cap with a feather. The way her husband's shoulder-length hair completed the costume, Bexley was certain she'd fight off virgin maidens all day.

The family of three had visited Temperance

Rose's estate so many times that Bexley half expected the car to make the journey on its own. Autopilot would've been helpful as Brewer spent more time gazing at her in the passenger's seat than watching the road.

Before long, his hand became deeply embedded in the thick of her curled hair, and his fingers massaged her scalp. "How do you expect me to keep my hands to myself?" he all but growled.

"That should be a no-brainer, considering we're headed to your ten-year-old niece's party." She gripped his firm bicep beneath the costume while rolling her eyes. "Would you quit staring? You're beginning to give me a complex."

"Hard not to—I've only seen you in a dress a few times. And that one…" He let out a low whistle as his eyes dusted over her bust. "Can hardly wait to undo those buckles later."

She glanced down at the bodice and grimaced. "All these buckles were hard to fasten. I'm not sure they'll loosen too easily. You might have to cut them off."

Brewer made a choking noise and almost missed the turn into Temperance's driveway, where iron-clad "knights" stood guard at the gate. "Damn it,

Squires. Keep talking like that, and I'll drag you back home."

Absentmindedly, Bexley laughed. She couldn't help wondering if he'd ever stop calling her "Squires," even once the name change was official. Would a piece of paper really change anything?

With the site of Temperance's sprawling estate on the other side of the gate, Captain inserted his head between them and released a sharp bark. He'd become best friends with Temperance's dog and tended to go crazy every time they were reunited. The second Brewer parked, Bexley opened her door, and Captain shot out of the backseat with the speed of a bullet, knocking his hat to one side of his head. Once Brewer and Bexley gathered Olive's presents from the trunk, they headed beyond the 3-story mansion that perfectly suited the Medieval theme with its turrets and elegant landscaping.

The already whimsical backyard had been transformed into a wonderland worthy of real-life royalty. Long tables adorned with more flowers than Bexley had seen in one place, and elegant china were arranged in the center of the yard. More "knights" roamed the property on black horses with rubber swords. Court jesters and handmaidens served elaborately dressed partygoers. Bexley recognized several movie stars and famous musicians, while many others had been her clients.

Before they could find Temperance or Olive, Bexley's sister and infant nephew joined them. Between Cineste's whimsical velvet dress, dark hair styled in complicated braids, and her nephew's powder-blue cape with matching balloon breeches, double-buttoned vest, and plume in a matching hat, they looked as if they'd just stepped off a movie set. Easton's wavy brown hair had grown down to his ears, and his costume brought out the same stunning color of his eyes. Bexley was convinced her sister should pimp him out as a baby model to start funding his college education.

"Look at this little prince!" Bexley exclaimed, feathering a finger along his jaw until he responded with a gummed smile and a gurgled coo. She nudged Brewer. "Just look at him!"

"I feel you, little man," Brewer told his nephew scandalously, snagging him from his mother's arms. Cradled in the crook of his muscular arms, the baby looked doll-sized. "The things we do for the women we love…just you wait."

Bexley's stomach clenched. Although her husband was somehow even more handsome when holding a baby, she was beyond grateful the child wasn't theirs. The love she felt for her nephew was overwhelming. Still, she wouldn't want to be solely responsible for teaching him the world's ways and ensuring he thrived in every other way. Trying to sustain Twila's landscaping around the cottage was enough of a struggle.

"I'm never going to hear the end of it when Alex sees what you're wearing," Cineste told Brewer with a dramatic roll of her eyes. "My husband is wearing a costume identical to his son's."

Brewer laughed in the gruff kind of way that made Bexley giddy. "Better brace yourself for the fallout because here comes your husband now."

Giggling behind her hand, Bexley watched with amusement as her brother-in-law joined them in the same powder-blue costume as his infant son. Considering Alex and Brewer had bonded over their veteran status, it was extra comical when Alex appeared ready to slug him. "Oh, come on, man! You have to be kidding me! If you weren't holding my son right now…"

"You'd what, Squid Boy?" Brewer challenged in the same playful tone. "Beat me to death with that feather in your hat?"

With a gleam in his eye, Alex seemed to be fighting against a smirk. "You know what? That costume is exactly what I'd expect to see a *Puddle Pirate* wearing."

The two men laughed and bumped fists. "What does a sailor gotta do to get a beer around here?" Alex asked, kissing his son's cheek.

"I don't know," Brewer answered, "but as a bonafide *Puddle Pirate*, I believe it's my duty to keep a *Swabbie* like *you* safe from harm." Chuckling, Brewer handed Easton back to Cineste and turned to kiss Bexley. "Don't go stealin' any hearts while I'm gone, Robin Hood," he whispered directly into her ear.

He delivered a hard smack to her rear before strutting away, eliciting a quiet yelp from her lips. Along with her sister, Bexley watched intently as the two men breached the crowd. The tailored pants fit Brewer's rear end like a luxurious glove.

"Wow," Cineste sighed dreamily. "I know he's your husband and everything because I have to remind myself of that fact every time he's around, but I gotta say—"

"What is Tabitha Torres doing here?" Bexley interrupted.

As the news anchor stepped in Brewer's way, eliciting one of his dimpled smiles, Bexley's stomach plummeted. Tabitha's bright blue body-con dress highlighted her every curve, making her stand out among those appropriately dressed for the occasion. Brewer didn't know the details of Jack's case or Tabitha's connection and seemed okay with engaging in conversation. Bexley was confident her husband wouldn't do anything to make her jealous. Still, she worried Tabitha may have followed them there, hoping to threaten Bexley on another level.

Shrugging, Cineste shot her a curious look. "Temperance asked her to come. She thought it would be good exposure to make the general public realize shelters are in dire need of funding." Easton fussed a little louder as she moved him over to rest on her other hip. "Do you have something against her?"

"I haven't decided," Bexley grumbled.

"I think Easton is getting hungry," her sister announced. "I'm going to slip inside to feed him. Wanna come with?"

Bexley shook her head and tried her hand at an English accent. "I think I shall stay here and keep watch over the kingdom."

Cineste gave a nasally laugh. "Whatever, weirdo."

Once her sister was gone, Bexley watched as Temperance and Olive—both wearing what had to have been the most elaborate gowns in existence—stepped in to hug Brewer. Her heart swelled when Olive leaped into Brewer's arms like a little monkey. He was so good with kids that Bexley worried she was depriving him of his right to become a father.

The tension began to release from Bexley's shoulders. Although she had every right to be paranoid after Tabitha's hostile visit to Stronghold Investigations, it made sense that Tabitha would want to cover the party. Beneath the sun's mildly powerful rays, Bexley took a deep breath, telling herself to relax.

Then, as she scanned the property to appreciate the hundreds of partygoers gathered in the most epic display of cosplay she'd ever witnessed, she spotted Jack strolling in from the front yard.

CHAPTER SIX

Jack Squires donned a proper prince costume, complete with a gold brocade jacket, a wide leather belt over black pants, and tall boots. He tugged on the blouse collar and glanced around the lavish property with unease as his short, golden hair ruffled in the wind from the nearby ocean. As Bexley closed in on him, she couldn't help musing how lucky her ex-husband would make another woman one day if he were to remarry. Over dinner the other night, he'd told Brewer that he hadn't had time for a serious relationship since his career had taken off.

"Jack!" Bexley called out, waving to grab his attention before he discovered Tabitha. She was certain nothing good would come out of a reunion between them. Arguing with her in front of hundreds of witnesses wouldn't do his career any favors, and she worried he'd accidentally say something to strengthen her lawsuit.

His bright blue eyes filled with relief once they found her. "Bexley?" He stepped in to kiss her cheek and squeeze her elbow. "You look great! What are you doing here?"

"Temperance Rose is a good friend of mine," she explained. "And the daughter she adopted, well…that's a long story. I guess you could say I'm Olive's honorary aunt." She briefly glanced over her shoulder at the crowd. "What are *you* doing here, *Prince* Squires?"

"I was invited by a colleague. He claims this friend of yours throws exceptional fundraisers that are well worth the price tag." He watched with wide eyes as one of the elaborately dressed "knights" trotted on a horse past them. "I guess he wasn't kidding."

"Temperance has a heart the size of Texas. She recently sold a fleet of luxury cars and gave the proceeds to various charities." Bexley nudged him around so his back was to Tabitha. "I'll introduce you to her as soon as we get you an ale. I promise she'll appreciate the effort you put into that costume."

When a chorus of laughter rang out, including a familiar gruff voice, Jack strained to look off into the distance beyond the hoards of attendees. "Wait, is that Brewer?"

Blocking his line of vision, Bexley released a frustrated breath. "It is, but you'll have to put your bromance on the back burner for now. You're not going over there."

"Why not?"

"He's talking to Tabitha, Jack."

Redness blossomed across his cheeks as his eyes narrowed. "What? *Why?* What the hell is she doing here?"

"Temperance asked her to cover the party to raise awareness for her cause. Brewer stumbled across her by accident. As you're perfectly aware, after our conversation the other night over dinner, he doesn't know Tabitha is behind the lawsuit." Bexley and Jack had agreed to keep the celebrity news anchor's identity concealed from Bexley's friends and family.

Shaking his head with determination, Jack started in their direction. "Maybe if I talk to her, face-to-face—"

Bexley gently pushed him back. "Look around you, Jack. Does this seem a good place to cause a scene? I told you she seemed fired up about her claims when she stopped by to see me yesterday morning. Nothing about her behavior makes me believe she'd be rational with you."

"What do you expect me to do, Bex? Run out of here with my tail between my legs?"

"No, but you should definitely lay low. Why don't you head inside? I'll bring the host in to meet you and explain the situation—if that's alright. Temperance has the biggest heart of anyone I know. I'm sure she can help us out of this sticky situation."

With a single nod and a reluctant glance back at Tabitha, Jack shuffled in the direction Bexley pointed, his head hung like a scolded child.

As Bexley started for her husband, a broad-shouldered man in a clunky knight's costume bumped her shoulder. Brushing his shaggy hair away from his bloodshot eyes, he threw her a dimpled smile. "Sorry, sweetheart."

As she looked into his emerald eyes, Bexley gasped. She knew those eyes and that dimpled smile. The former chef from the La Belle restaurant had been on her radar ever since he tried swindling a valuable pair of earrings that had disappeared at one of Kiersten's fashion shows. He was not only a borderline genius; he'd become quite wealthy and would've been able to afford the required donation to attend the party. But last Bexley had heard from him, Travis Paxton was fleeing the country with a hefty loot.

"Travis, what—"

"You never saw me, hot detective lady," he whispered, throwing her a wink before blending in with the crowd.

Still rattled from bumping into the genius con artist, Bexley sidled next to Brewer.

"Here's my gorgeous wife now!" he announced, pulling her close and dropping a soft kiss against her cheek.

Satisfaction roared through Bexley as the beautiful news anchor's dark eyes popped wide in surprise. Perhaps she even caught a spark of jealousy. *Let her eat cake*, Bexley thought to herself amidst a grin.

"You look *deslumbrante!*" Temperance gushed, clapping her hands together. "*¡Ay dios mío!*"

"Simmer down, Queen Rose," Bexley responded. "Everyone here would agree that you and your beautiful daughter are the most *deslum-*

brante royalty at this party." She bent to tap Olive's nose and threw her a genuine smile. "Seriously, you become more beautiful and mature with every day that goes by. Are you sure you're not one of Temperance's costars?"

Olive responded with a toothy grin. "You always ask me that, silly! I'm her *daughter* now!"

Bexley feigned surprise, bracing a hand over her lips. "Oh, that's right! How could I forget?" She bent to kiss the top of her niece's intricately braided head. "I can't wait for you to open your presents, Princess Olive."

Once she stood upright, Brewer tightened his muscular arm around her waist. "Bex, this is——"

"We've had the immense *pleasure* of meeting once already," Bexley assured him, turning her head sharply to give Tabitha a tight-lipped smile. "Hello, Miss Torres."

"Miss Squires," Tabitha all but spat in reply.

"Actually, it's *Mrs. Hawkins* now," Bexley replied before nudging her stunned husband with her hip. "I need a few minutes alone with Temp. Suppose you can guard Princess Sassy Pants while we're away?"

"Hey!" Olive squealed in reply.

Brewer recovered from Bexley's bombshell a

beat later with a playful smirk before bending at the waist and swirling one arm through the air. "I shall swear my allegiance to Princess Olive, my love." He brushed his lips over Bexley's cheek again, then held a bent arm out to Olive. "Shall we take a stroll among the pheasants, m'lady?"

Olive let out a high-pitched giggle before hooking her little arm around his. "You're so *weird*, Uncle Hawk!"

Slipping her arm through Temperance's, Bexley shot Tabitha a triumphant glance. "If you'll excuse us, my friend and I must tend to an urgent matter." She caught a flash of annoyance in the anchor's eyes before Bexley spun Temperance around, guiding her toward her mansion.

"Everything okay, *amiga*?" Temperance asked.

"I'm not sure how well you know miss big-shot back there, but she's bad news," Bexley told her. "Be very mindful of what you say when in her presence."

"I have years of experience with *serpientes* just like Tabitha Torres. I know how to charm someone in her position for the right reasons."

Bexley had no doubt.

In the few minutes that followed, Bexley gave her friend an abbreviated version of Jack and

Tabitha's story. After they breezed through the French doors together, Bexley spotted Jack sitting at the bottom of the grand stairway leading up to the second level. He stared down at the glass of beer in his hand with a forlorn expression.

"That's him," Bexley whispered. She watched as Temperance's dark eyes widened on Jack. A beat later, her elegant lips parted with a silent sigh. If Bexley didn't know better, Tabitha Torres had been right to claim Jack had a way of putting women "under a spell."

"Jack, this is Temperance Rose," Bexley announced.

Grinning, Jack shot to his feet and reached for Temperance's hand, pressing a kiss on its backside. "You failed to tell me your friend was a bonafide queen," he playfully scolded Bexley.

Temperance appeared too flustered to speak as her cheeks flushed dark red.

"Nice touch, *Romeo*," Bexley told him with a heavy dose of sarcasm. "But this is the wrong party, and that's the wrong costume."

Jack continued holding Temperance's hand. Neither of them seemed eager to break the connection. "Thank you for letting me crash your elaborate soirée, Miss Rose. When Travis Morello told me about it, I wanted to get in on the noble cause."

"*Gracias*, Mr. Squires," Temperance replied, void of her usual charm. "That was kind of you. But please, call me Temperance."

His grin grew. "And you can call me Jack."

Bexley stopped herself from rolling her eyes. After all, who was she to stand in their way if they felt a connection? "About our little problem outside…you know, the vixen in ridiculously high heels that don't match the vibe of her costume—"

"I've decided it would be best if I head out," Jack interrupted, finally releasing Temperance's hand when addressing Bexley. "Tabitha is here to spread awareness of Temperance's good deed, and I wouldn't want to get in the way of that." His gaze swung back onto Temperance. "However, I would be honored if I could have the pleasure of taking you out to dinner some night so you can tell me more about your other deeds as a humanitarian. Bexley tells me you have an extremely kind soul."

In an unusual act of shyness, Temperance dropped her chin. "Miss Bexley is too kind herself. But I would be honored to accompany you to dinner, Jack. I only need enough notice to make arrangements for my daughter."

"You know she's always welcome at our house," Bexley reminded her.

Jack's face lit with excitement. "If it's alright with you, I'll get your number from Bexley and call you later this week to make arrangements."

"I would love that," Temperance gushed.

Bexley stepped closer to Jack and motioned to the other side of the house. "I'll walk you out."

Jack again took Temperance's hand and brushed his lips over the backside. "I will look forward to seeing you again, my queen."

Giggling much like Olive, Temperance lifted the sides of her dress before giving him an expertly executed curtsy. "As will I, m'Lord."

Snorting, Bexley gripped Jack's arm and all but dragged him away. "Could you be any more obviously smitten?" she whispered. "How did I not remember how much you lack in the art of subtlety?"

"Can you blame me?" he fired back. "She's stunning, and her commitment to causes like the Humane Society makes her even more attractive."

A maternal-like instinct tugged at Bexley's insides. "Whatever ends up happening between the two of you, you better not hurt her. If you think

Tabitha Torres is a festering sore on your back, just wait until you make me angry."

Jack glanced her way with a growing smirk. "I forgot how you get kind of hot when you're all fired up."

Bexley grabbed a handful of his blouse to stop him. "I mean it, Jack. They don't come as nice as her—she's irreplaceable. You'll have to be careful. Whatever happens with Tabitha's lawsuit better not affect Temperance in any way. She's too good of a soul to become a target to an evil T.V. celebrity with a grudge."

"I promise to be discreet," he said, all at once somber. "I would be just as upset if Tabitha sunk her claws into Temperance. I won't let that happen."

"That's what I like to hear." Bexley released her grip on his costume and patted his arm. "In the meantime, I promise to do everything I can to uncover Tabitha's motives. Hopefully, we can resolve the issue soon, and this mess will be far behind us."

CHAPTER SEVEN

Although it was a Sunday and Bexley had promised her husband she would stick to an 8-5 schedule during the weekdays, she slumped behind the steering wheel of her Expedition as Tabitha Torres drove a shiny new, white BMW through her property's grand gates. After a beat, Bexley pulled out onto the road behind her. The annoyance of finding the evil temptress at Temperance's party—if she was being honest, had escalated after witnessing her attempt to flirt with Brewer—had festered overnight, making it impossible for Bexley to let the case slide any until Monday morning.

Besides, Red had secured a copy of Tabitha's schedule, and following the anchor to and from the station during the work week could be pointless. Bexley would most likely catch her doing something memorable during her leisure time.

They were only a few blocks from Tabitha's home when the Expedition's dashboard screen alerted her to an incoming call from Deputy Danks.

Bexley tapped the answer button. "To what do I owe this pleasure, Deputy?"

"Did you hear about the woman that was murdered earlier this week?" he asked.

"I saw the headlines but didn't have time to read the article. Why? What's the story?"

"Strangulation of a single white female in her mid-thirties, middle-class. No leads, but I found a piece of what I believe to be crucial evidence tucked inside her pocket. I've been sitting on it for a few days, waiting for Sheriff Blair to approve more resources to look into it further, but he seems to think it's nothing."

"You mean to say our elected sheriff isn't doing his job?" she replied with an artificial gasp. "Say it isn't so!"

"I was wondering if you could meet up with me so I could bounce some ideas off of you. I'm hoping to impress the PS chief, so he'll take me seriously when I apply for detective now that Grayson Rivers has left town."

When her one-time boyfriend's name was mentioned, Bexley felt a hollow pang in her chest. She took a slow breath while activating her blinker to turn the corner behind Tabitha's vehicle. "I promised Brewer I wouldn't work on the weekends."

"Oh yeah? What are you doing now?"

Bexley glanced over her shoulder, expecting to find a sheriff's cruiser nearby. "Are you following me, Deputy?"

"No, but I can tell you're in your vehicle, and I don't hear Hawkins or your dog. We both know that getting your nails done or cruising the mall aren't activities you'd waste your weekend doing."

"Well played, Deputy. You're already thinking like a detective." Huffing, she lifted her foot off the accelerator as Tabitha parked at the front curb of a sizable non-profit gym. "Let me finish my current *errand*, and I'll let you know once I'm free."

After she ended the call, she craned her neck to watch a young blond-haired boy in gym shorts and a T-shirt with sneakers skip in front of Tabitha's car before sliding into the front seat. It was most peculiar, considering Red had stated the news anchor to be childless. She supposed it could be the son of a friend or relative.

Then the boy looked over his shoulder while securing his seatbelt, and Bexley gasped.

With the blast of a car horn, she swung her gaze back to the street. Her breaths came out in jaded huffs once she realized she had almost side-swiped a vehicle in the next lane.

The boy looked nearly identical to the pictures she'd seen of her ex-husband at a similar age.

It was downright delusional to conclude Jack and the boy weren't related.

Bexley decided she'd deal with Deputy Danks before deciding how to handle the situation with Tabitha and Jack. While it was slightly possible she had only imagined the boy's resemblance to Jack, she had a sinking feeling that wasn't the case. She didn't want to think about how devastated her ex-husband would be to discover he had an older child he knew nothing about. The best course of action would be confronting Tabitha head-on—when she would least expect an ambush.

The baby-faced deputy waved her down from a

booth when she entered the quaint diner on the outskirts of Papaya Springs, where the ostentatious mansions and their mostly corrupt occupants resided miles away. She wasn't surprised to discover him wearing jeans, a T-shirt, and a ball cap pulled down to his bright green eyes since she hadn't seen a cruiser in the parking lot. Apparently, she wasn't the only one working off the clock.

"Does your girlfriend know you're here?" she asked as she slid into the booth across from him. "Or should I have come incognito, too?"

"Angie knows I'm meeting with you," he assured her, eyes darting across the diner as if worried someone was listening. "She isn't too happy about it, but at least she likes you. I'm more worried about the sheriff getting wind of our meeting."

She nodded, agreeing he was absolutely right. If the sheriff found out his deputy was consulting with her, he make his life a living hell. He'd stoop as low as straight-up firing Danks and tainting his reputation.

A waitress appeared to fill the coffee cup waiting upside down in front of Bexley. Despite feeling exhausted from the past few days' events, Bexley pushed it away once the waitress was gone. The dark coffee's strong aroma made her stomach churn.

Folding her hands on the table, she met Deputy Danks's gaze. "So what's this piece of evidence in question?"

"There was a note left at the crime scene. I meant to consult with you earlier, but I got caught up in the case and forgot about reaching out. Then I heard about the call the sheriff took to your neighbor's house the other night involving a second dead mouse, and I began to suspect there could be a connection." He retrieved something from his lap, then passed her a torn piece of paper inside an evidence bag. "I'd like to know your take on it."

Bexley studied the handwritten note.

Your Next, My Little Mouse

Blowing out a calming breath, her hands began to shake. The reference to mice shook her to her core. "My take is whoever wrote this most likely didn't graduate high school. They didn't use the proper spelling of *you're*." She held the note off to the side. "Has Forensic seen this?"

"They only extracted a partial thumbprint from the victim. It would make sense she would've touched it as there was a notebook in one of her kitchen drawers with a piece torn out matching this one. The killer must've been wearing gloves."

"What did they say about the handwriting?"

"Sheriff Blair didn't think pursuing it was important enough to use taxpayers' money." The deputy removed his ball cap to scratch his dark hair. "Do you think it could be some kind of threat to another intended victim? Maybe even that neighbor of yours?"

"Absolutely. I imagine the killer wrote this hoping it would be leaked to the media." *So Twila would get the message*, she silently confirmed with a sickening feeling gnawing at her gut. She didn't want to get the deputy too fired up until she knew more. "Do you care if I take a picture? I'd keep the image safe."

The deputy's tongue slipped out to wet his lips. "I suppose that would be alright. Just as long as you remember my job is on the line."

"I know it is, and I appreciate your efforts." Bexley angled her phone's camera at the bag, first disengaging the flash. "I'll protect it with my life."

Bexley raced home, cutting through traffic and breaking numerous laws that could potentially land her in jail for reckless driving. A part of her hoped the writing and the nickname on the note would both be unfamiliar to Twila, and it was merely a freak coincidence that someone was leaving dead mice on the kind old woman's step. But Bexley knew better.

Her heart plummeted when she saw Jack's black Tesla pulling into their driveway mere seconds ahead. She'd been hoping to address the Tabitha situation after she'd had a chance to either confirm or deny that the child was Jack's. Keeping the revelation from her old friend would be impossible.

She parked her Expedition and sprang out onto the driveway before Jack could start for the house. She sensed it would be better if Brewer wasn't around to witness Jack's reaction to her revelation.

Jack was dressed for a leisurely day in a crisp white polo shirt and khaki shorts. His lean and muscular calves and feet inside leather sandals were so ghostly white that Bexley doubted he'd spent any casual time outside since moving to California.

When he smiled, the gleam in his blue eyes and

the flash of his perfectly spaced teeth made Bexley experience a new layer of guilt for the news she was about to break. With a pang of nostalgia, she remembered a time when those teeth had been encased in braces.

"Can't be a successful sports broadcaster without a perfect smile," he once declared back when they were broke students attending NYU. He had sold the classic, albeit rusted-out Mustang his grandfather had willed to him in order to cover the expense of tuition—and the braces.

"Guess where I'm headed?" he asked. "I'll give you a hint—it has everything to do with a beautiful Latina. We're keeping it casual for the first date… playing tennis at her place, then having ice cream with her daughter afterward."

Bexley couldn't force a smile in return. She almost regretted leaving Brewer out of the conversation as she could've drawn on his strength at that moment. "Jack, we need to talk."

"You don't have to worry, Bex. I promise to be a perfect gentleman—"

"Jack," she interrupted in the most gentle voice she could muster, "I think you might be a father."

He leaned back against the side of his Tesla and paled, chin dropping to his chest. For a moment,

Bexley was worried he might pass out cold. She prayed she was right and wasn't putting him through the shock for nothing.

"I followed Tabitha this morning," she explained, moving in closer in case she had to catch him. "She picked up a blonde little boy, probably around ten years old. I didn't have a chance to see him up close, and he only looked my way for a moment, but…Jack, he looked *just* like you did as a kid. I wouldn't tell you this if I wasn't certain of the resemblance."

Jack slowly drew his head back upright before his troubled gaze landed on hers.

"I was hoping it wasn't true."

CHAPTER EIGHT

Attempting to wrap her head around her ex-husband's shocking disclosure, Bexley blinked several times before she was able to speak. "You *knew* you may have fathered a child with Tabitha?" It was hard to keep the bitterness out of her voice. "Don't you think you should've mentioned that when you first hired me?"

Jack combed a hand through his dark hair. "I think a part of me wanted to pretend it couldn't be true. Verbalizing my suspicions to you only would've made the possibility more tangible."

Huffing, she leaned against his car beside him and crossed her arms over her chest, glancing down at her feet. "*Ignoring* the possibility wasn't going to make it go away."

"I had an inkling back in the day," he said, sounding as sad as she'd ever heard him. "One of the friends I'd interned with said she'd put on some weight after I left. When I ran into the network's field producer, she told me Tabitha had been let go because she called in sick at least once weekly. That's around when she stepped away from the spotlight for a while. At one point, I guessed she had disappeared long enough to have a child and that it might even be mine. Then, she was held captive by her sister's husband, and her story went nationwide. If there had been a kid in her life, they would've mentioned it at some point, but they kept referring to her as a single woman. I don't know if you watched any of that unfold, but extensive interviews were given, and she left nothing on the table. I watched every last one to ensure I didn't miss anything."

"I don't get it," Bexley told him. "My assistant dug into Tabitha's history. There wasn't any mention of her being pregnant or having a child."

Jack winced. "Do I want to know what other felonious means you've used in my case?"

Ignoring the question, Bexley focused on an idea. She turned to face her first husband head-on. "There are some career women who don't have time or interest in a child—she's vain enough to think it would tarnish her image. She's *devious* enough to hide something as monumental as childbirth. She could've paid off a doctor—delivered the baby privately and falsified the birth record with a bogus name."

"If that were the case, don't you think she would've given it—*him*—up for adoption? Why would she pick him up from a public gym ten years later?"

"Good point," Bexley agreed. As she tapped a finger against her chin, a new idea clicked into place: "Or *maybe* she forged the birth records so the child legally belonged to someone close to her—someone she could visit on her own terms, someone she could claim to be a relative without bearing the responsibility of motherhood."

One of Jack's eyebrows curved. "You mean like a nephew?"

"It's a possibility," she decided with an enthusiastic nod. "First thing Monday morning, I'll arrange to speak with the sister. She may not be willing to spill any tea on Tabitha, but I've become a pretty good lie detector. I can feel her out…hopefully even get a glance of her 'son' and see if it's the same boy." Unable to look him in the eye when she asked her next question, she glanced down as her fingers picked at imaginary lint on her shorts. "What if this kid really is yours? Do you think you'd want to be involved in his life?" It was a highly personal question to ask someone she hadn't been close with in a long time.

"You know what? I think so," he decided. "I mean, it would suck that I missed out on watching him grow up for the first part of his life, but I'm in a good place right now. I could provide him with everything he could ever want or need."

"If you mean financial support, I think Tabitha would already have that covered."

"I'm talking about giving him a *real* family. At the very least, I could be a father figure. Considering Tabitha's brother-in-law is in prison, there might not be any male influences in his life."

Bexley gently nudged him in his side. "It blows my mind to think you might be a *dad*. Next thing you know, you'll be sporting New Balances and outdated cargo shorts."

He chuckled. "I've always wanted to have kids. I was just waiting for the right woman to come along."

"Not me," she said to him. "You know my childhood was less than ideal. And the thought of being responsible for another human's well-being is suffocating. Brewer and I are happy with the way things are. I know he'd make the best dad if I changed my mind, but he says he doesn't want kids either."

"Bex," Jack replied, his voice soft, "It's obvious that man worships the ground you walk on. Are you sure he isn't merely going along with the decision not to have kids for your benefit?"

Her throat tightened. Even though Hawk had assured her endless times that children weren't on his radar after seeing him interact with their niece and nephew, her greatest fear was that he'd been lying. *He* had been worried that he wasn't enough for *her*. What if it was the other way around? There was very little she wouldn't do for the man she loved unconditionally. Still, she didn't think she had it in her to start a family only to appease him.

She cleared her throat. "If that boy is yours, it still doesn't explain the lawsuit. Even if she wasn't independently wealthy, it's not like she needs child support."

"Like you've said before, maybe she's just bitter."

"I'm convinced there's something bigger at play," she insisted, shaking her head.

"I'm certain that you'll figure it out, whatever it

is." Jack moved away from the vehicle, so Bexley followed suit. "I better get going. I just wanted to stop by and let you know about my date with Temperance before you hear it from her. I know you have a lot going on these days, so I wanted to assure you there's nothing to worry about regarding my possible involvement with your friend. At this point, we're merely getting to know each other. I'll let you know if and when that changes. And I sure as hell won't let my intentions with her go beyond you and Hawk until Tabitha backs down." He dropped a kiss on her cheek before he slipped into his car.

Bexley stood in the driveway, throwing him a little wave as he pulled into their street. It was touching that he'd thought it necessary to stop by and fill her in on his date, and she was relieved that he'd taken the news of his suspected offspring so well. More than anything, however, she was unnerved by his question.

"Are you sure he isn't merely going along with the decision not to have kids for your benefit?"

Behind the cottage, Brewer, wearing nothing more than a wet suit hanging from his hips, chucked the ball to Cap while ankle-deep in water. Brewer's hair and Cap's coat glistened with moisture from a recent dip in the ocean, and Brewer's surfboard was wedged upright in the sand behind them. Bexley stopped to watch them momentarily, breathing in the brine of the saltwater while battling her conflicted feelings. She was the luckiest girl in the world to have won the former bad boy's heart when he could've had his pick of any woman. Shouldn't she feel obligated to make him happy with his choice to be with her, no matter the cost?

Cap spotted her and came leaping through the sand, greeting her with kisses. Grinning, Brewer came right behind him to do the same. She swooned on her feet with her husband's talented lips sweeping against hers.

"You said you'd only be gone for a short while," he scolded as he wrapped his strong arms around her head, making Bexley feel like a teenage girl crushing on the school's bad boy. His bare chest was still cool from the water, and the neoprene was still damp. "We had an agreement, Squires."

"You're going to have to come up with a new nickname for me now that we share the same last name," she teased, wiggling her eyebrows. "If you start calling me Hawk, I'm going to assume you're simply conversing with yourself. And that would only fuel my theory that you've hit your head one time too many."

His face lit with pure joy as his eyebrows shot upward. "About that…we never got a chance to talk about it. Did you only say that for that reporter lady's sake?"

Shaking her head, she could not help but match his wide grin. "I sent an application in to get it changed a few days ago. I'm not entirely convinced I'll use Hawkins for work, though. Whether good or bad, I've made a name for myself in Papaya Springs."

"What made you change your mind?"

"I decided I wanted the bragging rights," she teased, rising on her toes to steal another kiss. "Or maybe it's the human equivalent of a dog marking its territory…who knows. I can't seem to think straight when I'm around you."

"You're still not off the hook," he grumbled, removing his arms from around her head to brush away strands of hair that had blown around her face. "You know I'd never tell you what you should or shouldn't do, but I hate to see you slip back into the habit of working too hard like you did when I was away. And a part of me is worried you'll be too exhausted to spend quality time with your husband at the end of the day. Especially when it seems you've been more tired than usual. Call me selfish, but I enjoy every minute we spend together."

Her expression softened along with her heart. "I do, too, Hawk. You know that." She glanced down to trace the elaborate "B" inked over his heart. "I realize we've talked about this *ad nauseam*, but is what we have enough for you? I mean, *are* we enough?"

"Did *you* hit your head?" he asked, biting back on a smirk as he mocking rubbed the back of her skull. "Where's *this* coming from? Is this because I was holding little E-man the other day?" He framed her face in his hands. "You and me…babe, it's more than I could've asked for. When Izzy and the baby died…" he paused when his voice cracked with pain. "It nearly destroyed me. I didn't think I'd ever recover."

"I know, babe," Bexley whispered, stroking a hand over the stubble on his jaw.

"It's enough that I'm always worrying about you getting hurt while on the job. I don't think I'd have the strength to worry about losing another child.

And I agree with you—I wouldn't want the kind of responsibility that comes with being a parent. I like our carefree lifestyle. I would resent the kid for being saddled into teacher conferences and endless hours in a gymnasium."

"It's just…Jack was just here a minute ago. I may have discovered he's a father, and we got into this whole conversation about being parents. He put this idea in my head that maybe you only agreed with me because it's what *I* want."

Brewer shook his head and winced. "First off, the guy should mind his own business because he couldn't be more wrong. And secondly, *what?*"

"Part of the reason I'm late is because I followed Tabitha Torres for a little while this morning," she confessed. "She's behind the sexual harassment suit against him."

Brewer stepped back to run a hand through his wet hair. "That's…wow."

"Wait, it gets better. I saw her with a young boy this morning who resembled Jack. When I told him about the kid, he confessed he knew it was possible. We talked it over, and I have a sneaking suspicion that Tabitha hid the fact that she had a kid by giving him to her sister to raise."

His eyebrows rose. "That's messed up. But what

does any of that have to do with the ridiculous claims against him?"

"I'm not sure. I told him I'll be looking into it on Monday."

"And I have no doubt you'll get to the bottom of her intentions." He nuzzled her neck. "You should go slip into that bikini I bought you last week. It'd be a good time to continue with those surf lessons."

Flutters arose in her chest. She loved their one-on-one sessions almost as much as she loved Pollo's tacos. "I wish I could, but there's something vital I need to do."

He drew back with a scowl. "Work-related?"

"Deputy Danks asked me to meet him after I followed Tabitha," she explained with a heavy sigh. "I need to talk to Twila about the evidence he found at a recent murder scene. I'm afraid it might have something to do with those dead mice on her step—maybe even the intruder." Gazing into his beautiful eyes, she fought past the nagging fear that built up after meeting with Deputy Danks. "I think she might be in serious danger, Hawk."

Twila grasped Bexley's phone with a hand covered in dried paint. She'd been working on the final piece for her upcoming art show when they'd knocked on her door. Frowning, she handed Bexley's phone back. "Sure, I dated a man who called me by that same nickname," she admitted with a shrug. "But that was decades ago. We were just kids."

"What was his name?" Bexley asked, exchanging a concerned look with Brewer.

"Arnold," she answered, suddenly seeming miles away when her eyes fixated on nothing. She stroked Cap's head when he obediently sat at her side. "Arnold Douglas."

Bexley typed the name into her phone's notepad designated for Twila's case. Hopefully, Brewer would understand when she dedicated the rest of the day to digging into the man's history. "What can you tell me about him?"

"He was a big man with large hands." She let out a content sigh and tilted her head off to one side. "A generous lover."

Brewer, who had showered and changed into dry clothes before accompanying Bexley, attempted to cover a sudden bout of laughter with a violent cough.

"That's wonderful for you," Bexley replied, her voice oozing with sarcasm, "but what did this man do for a living? How did you meet him? Where was he from?"

Twila's clear blue eyes skipped between the married couple. "Have you two had lunch yet?"

"No," they answered in unison.

Bexley added, "But, Twila—"

"I'll make you something while I tell you everything I know about Arnold," the elderly woman insisted, rising from her chair to retrieve one of Cap's favorite treats. "It will be better if I have something to keep my hands busy while I tell you his story."

PART II

PART II

CHAPTER NINE
PAPAYA SPRINGS, CALIFORNIA

49 YEARS PRIOR

At twenty-two, Twila Finn embodied all the traits of what society at the time of her early childhood had been quick to label as "a hippie." She loved animals and nature, didn't believe in violence, embraced Buddhist philosophies, and wasn't opposed to the occasional joint to open her mind. Her golden blond hair had grown to her lower back, and she tended to wear it in complicated braids. Most of her dresses were sewn on the machine she'd inherited when her grandmother passed away, and she strung bright-colored beads to create unique jewelry she proudly displayed by the oodles. She was usually either seen barefoot or wearing minimalist leather sandals.

To her mother's dismay, she had hitchhiked her way all across the country over the past four years, meeting various musicians and artists who fed her soul and awakened her desire to paint. She often waitressed or babysat to make ends meet and took on passionate lovers in nearly every city she temporarily called home. She fell in and out of love so often that their names and faces blurred with time.

One of the traits she possessed that separated her from the stereotypical hippies of the prior decade was that she appreciated anyone who served their country. Both her father and one of her older brothers had died in the war, and the other remaining male in her family was a Captain in the Army, so she never supported the movements that involved spitting on soldiers and calling them awful names. Accordingly, it was unsurprising to anyone who knew her when she dated a soldier injured in Vietnam.

Their introduction had been serendipitous. She had returned to her hometown of Papaya Springs in California because her big brother, Tommy, was coming home from Vietnam as it was rumored the war was ending. The soldier who would become her next lover was stepping off the airport shuttle, and at the same time, she was on her tip-toes, looking for Tommy.

Twila didn't know it then, but the soldier was still learning how to maneuver with crutches after a spray of bullets had wedged inside his thigh. Luckily, the doctors had been able to clean his wound rather than resorting to amputation like they first thought. As a result of his clumsiness, one of his wayward crutches knocked Twila to the ground.

"Ma'am!" the soldier cried, tossing the crutches aside. He crouched down unsteadily, bracing one hand against the pavement. He towered over her like a mountain. "I'm so sorry, ma'am! Are you alright?"

Twila looked into his dark, russet eyes and felt a surge of what she thought at the time was undoubtedly love at first sight. He was a big man with broad shoulders and an intense nose on a masculine face. His sandy brown hair was neatly shaved on the sides like most soldiers she'd seen. He made the khaki uniform look better than any other soldier she'd met.

She giggled. "That's one way to sweep a girl off her feet!"

With an uneasy chuckle, the hulking man helped her to stand. "These damn crutches do more harm than good."

She quickly retrieved the crutches from the ground and handed them to him one at a time. "You were injured in 'Nam," she assumed, her soft voice reflecting the empathy blossoming in her chest.

He took one long look at her colorful skirt and cropped blouse revealing her slim belly before he let out a cross *humph*. "What's it to you?"

Behind him, her brother shouted her name. Squealing, she carefully maneuvered around the injured soldier and leaped into her brother's arms.

"I missed you, baby girl!" Tommy exclaimed, hugging her tight before setting her back on the ground. He flashed one of his crooked grins that she both adored and had missed like crazy. He was strikingly handsome in the Army's dress uniform with dozens of metals pinned to his chest.

Tommy, Twila's only surviving brother, was a mere eighteen months older. Still, she'd always considered him more of a parental figure—especially since their father had died. He had been a shoulder to cry on the first time a boy broke her heart and a patient tutor when she feared she would fail a science class. They'd exchanged dozens of letters while he'd been overseas, and he'd been a voice of reason whenever she'd questioned her destiny.

His blue eyes sparkled when he teased, "Did you grow a couple of inches while I was gone?"

"No, silly goose," she replied, slapping his hand away before he could tug on one of her braids. "I stopped growing a long time ago."

"You look great, sis. The gypsy life must be good to you." Her brother's bright grin faded as his eyes scanned the area. "Where's Mom?"

"She sent me to pick you up with her station wagon." Twila took care in straightening her brother's crooked tie. "You know how she felt about your decision to stay in the service, Tommy. She hates that you still wanted to leave after we lost Dad and Mike. But I'm sure she'll warm up to you after you've been back a day or two. You'll see."

Tommy glared at something over her shoulder. "What are you looking at, Douglas?"

"That's your sister?" the injured soldier asked.

"Don't even think about it," Tommy warned. "She's off limits."

With another cross *humph*, the soldier limped away, appearing uncoordinated with every swing of the crutches. Twila turned back to her brother and lightly slapped his chest.

"I can fend for myself. You didn't have to be so mean."

"I was doing you a favor." Tommy hooked an arm around her neck and guided her toward the luggage bay beneath the bus. "Arnold Douglas is a weirdo."

Twila would've scolded her brother for being unfairly mean if they had been younger. "Do you know what happened to him?"

Her brother released her to grab a large duffle bag with their last name stenciled on the side. As he slung the bag over his shoulder, he shrugged. "He was in a unit that was ambushed while sweeping the jungle for Charlie. It's a pretty common occurrence over there. He's just lucky to be alive."

Twila glanced back to discover the wounded soldier struggling to carry his duffle bag while operating the crutches.

"He needs help," she told her brother. "You may think he's weird, but he made a lot of sacrifices when he went to war, Tommy. Same as you."

Tommy shook his head repeatedly. "You haven't changed one bit, baby sister. Always with the bleeding heart for animals and the less fortunate."

With a bright chuckle, her brother nudged her toward the other soldier. "Come on. I'll carry his bag, and we'll help him get on his way."

As it turned out, Arnold Douglas didn't have a ride arranged from the bus station. He'd planned to hitchhike to the apartment he had rented via mail correspondence from a distant cousin. It had taken a lot of pleading before Twila convinced her brother to offer Arnold a ride.

Once they arrived at the address Arnold's cousin had given, Twila was horrified to think anyone would actually live there. The dilapidated apartment building was located on the north side of Papaya Springs, known for factories that had closed after the Second World War and an abandoned rail yard mostly occupied by bums. Only two cars occupied the parking space in front of the 2-story building: an old 50s Coupe and a 70-something Maverick. Based on the declining condition of the Coupe, in addition to a handful of weeds growing through the windows, it appeared to have been abandoned years ago. The Maverick was riddled with dents and a missing rear bumper.

The trio made their way up the rickety stairway to the second floor. The hallways were dark despite being light outside, and the stench of urine assaulted their noses. Twila was sure the other units were unoccupied as the thud of their footsteps and the creaking of the stairs were the only sounds to be heard. Twila carried Arnold's crutches while he limped up with one hand grasped on the railing, and Tommy lugged Arnold's bag in the rear. *How would Arnold go up and down the stairs on his own?* Twila worried.

In the second-floor hallway, Arnold stopped at the door marked 8. Faded red paint chipped the battered door, and the sagging brass handle creaked beneath Arnold's grip. Unsurprisingly, the door was unlocked. Twila sensed she wasn't the only one holding her breath as he nudged the door open.

The studio apartment featured an ancient olive-green stove and a stained twin mattress in the same cramped space. A threadbare curtain separated the space from a toilet, a pedestal sink, and a small shower head aimed over a plastic basin. Old crates were stacked on either side of the stove in place of kitchen cabinets, containing a single, rusted-out pan and a cracked dish. The outline of where a refrigerator once stood stained a blank wall.

At one point, Twila startled, certain she'd seen something scurrying along the floorboards from the corner of her eye. She had taken residence in many questionable places over the years while on her voyage across the country, including a barn in the Midwest. Still, nothing had been even close to that horrendous level. It was a far cry from the welcome home a wounded soldier deserved.

Her eyes watered as Tommy dropped the man's bag in the middle of the cracked linoleum floor and grunted. "This place is a real dump."

"Guess it explains why my cousin isn't charging much," Arnold replied, glancing around the accommodations.

"You can't stay *here!*" she cried, exhaling exasperatedly. "Surely this building is set to be condemned!"

"If you knew the conditions we sometimes faced back in 'Nam, you would realize it's not a big deal," Tommy told her while lighting a cigarette.

Arnold eyed the bed as if he'd been thinking the same thing as Twilia—*how would a man of his size fit on that tiny mattress?* "It just needs a little cleaning."

Tommy stuck a hand out for Arnold to shake. "Take care of yourself, man."

"We can't just leave him here!" Twila

exclaimed, her voice tight with oncoming tears. "The bed doesn't even have sheets!"

Laughing, Tommy blew out a plume of smoke. "It beats a wet jungle floor." He nudged Arnold with his elbow. "Ain't that right, brother?"

Twila noticed Arnold's complexion had turned a little green. "Nonsense," she insisted. "He's coming home with us for dinner and staying in the spare bedroom until this place is properly ready. I'll take him by the thrift store in the morning for sheets, a pillow, and whatever other basic necessities he'll need. I don't care where you two slept in 'Nam. This is not acceptable."

Tommy took another drag from his cigarette before he tipped his head at the ceiling. "Twila, *come on*. The man will be fine. Right, Douglas?"

"Don't be rude, Tommy!" she scolded, slapping her brother's arm.

Arnold appeared to be frozen in time, staring at Twila without blinking. She stepped forward to set her hand on top of one of his, still wrapped around a crutch. She attempted to flash him her sweetest smile. "I mean, if that's alright with you."

"I—I'd like that," he stammered. "A lot."

CHAPTER TEN

Losing a son and a husband within a year of each other had aged Lillian Finn and made her a hard woman. She was nothing like she'd been throughout Twila and Tommy's childhood. It had been part of the reason Twila had decided to leave home the day after graduating high school. As much as she loved her mother and tried to help her get past her grief, she couldn't stand being around her any longer.

When Twila breezed into the ranch-style home behind Arnold and her brother, their mother didn't rouse from the brown floral couch riddled with cigarette burns. She simply squinted her eyes, the same clear blue shade as her daughter's, while sucking on a cigarette.

"Who's the gimpy kid?" she demanded.

"Mom!" Twila scolded. "That isn't nice! He was hurt in the war!"

Arnold swallowed hard beside Twila. "M'name's Arnold Douglas, ma'am. Your daughter was kind enough to offer me a place to stay for the night until I can…well…"

"Get back on your feet?" Lillian supplied with a wry grin.

Tommy deposited the two military bags by the front door. "Good to see you, too, Momma," he mumbled as he headed toward her and dropped a kiss on her cheek. "I missed you."

Their mother said nothing in reply, just looked at him through a narrowed gaze. Tears stung Twila's eyes. Why was it so hard for their mother to show love for her only living son? She understood how hard it had been for Lillian to move on after her husband and oldest son had passed, but it was as if her remaining two children no longer meant anything without the rest of their family.

To hell with her, Twila thought, defiantly squaring her shoulders. "Tommy, go ahead and clean yourself up. I'll show Arnold to his room and start dinner. How do steaks and mashed potatoes sound?"

"Like heaven," Tommy declared with one of his biggest crooked grins.

"*His* room?" Lillian sneered, gritting her nicotine-stained teeth. "You mean *Timmy's* room? You're gonna let this *Neanderthal* stay in there?"

"It's not like Tim needs it," Tommy snapped before storming toward his childhood room.

Before their mom could spew any more cruel thoughts at them, Twila steered Arnold around to the hallway leading to the remaining bedrooms. She wiped the tears from her eyes, taking a shuttering breath once the bitter shell of a woman who had raised her was out of sight.

"Maybe I should get a motel room for the night," Arnold said quietly. "I don't want to be a burden to anyone."

"You're *not* a burden," Twila assured him with a sad little shake of her head. She leaned back against the paneled wall and smiled at him. "I wish you could've met her before my daddy and Timmy passed. Believe it or not, she was a lot of fun."

"She's very beautiful," he told her. "Just like her daughter."

Twila felt a little dizzy when she gazed into his dark eyes. Something about them drew her in, making her want to sink her fingers into the longer brown hair on the top of his head. For the first time in years, she felt the desire to paint a human instead of the usual landscapes and objects. She wasn't the best at painting faces, but she was determined to capture the sharp, unforgiving angles of Arnold's handsome face.

Her cheeks warmed with the sudden idea of standing on her tiptoes to kiss his broad lips. She wasn't usually shy around men and wondered what made this one so different.

She tugged on his sleeve. "Come on, I'll show you where you're sleeping. When Tommy's done with his shower, I'll have him bring your bag to you so you can freshen up. I'm sure you're sick of wearing that uniform."

Arnold called after her as she walked away, "Thank you for your kindness, Miss Twila."

Twila wasn't one bit surprised when their mother headed to bed the moment she was finished eating dinner. She hadn't offered to help Twila prepare the meal or clean up after, which was fine with Twila. Their mother had stopped cooking anything beyond microwaved meals since their father's passing, so Twila hadn't expected anything from her.

Everyone could breathe a little easier after Lillian left the room. They no longer had to watch everything they said to avoid offending or upsetting her, and the overall mood instantly brightened. Tommy put a Led Zeppelin vinyl on the turntable before sinking back into the chair across the table from his sister. In a striped T-shirt and blue jeans, he looked more like the brother she'd partied with in high school. He only missed the beautiful feathered hair they'd shaved off when he enlisted.

He grinned at Twila while lighting a fresh cigarette. "So tell me more about these adventures of yours, little sis. Your letters didn't tell me nearly enough about what you've been up to since I left."

"Like I told you, I started out in Florida," she told him with a dreamy sigh. "It was beautiful and warm, but not really my scene. I was only there for a few weeks before I made my way to upstate New York. It was pretty there, and I loved the ease of visiting the art galleries and museums in Manhattan whenever I wanted. But for some reason, it didn't feel like home. I always felt as if I were a tourist. Then, I met someone who convinced me to head to New Orleans with them, and I instantly fell in love with the city. I just knew I had to stay. The dreamy architecture was like nothing I'd ever seen, and the people were so friendly. And don't even get me started on the music…I fell head over heels for jazz! They have these amazing festivals and parades, especially around Mardi Gras. And the food—oh, *the food.* Tommy, it was *amazing!* I got the most amazing jambalaya recipe from a 90-year-old woman named Miss Penny. She became one of my very dearest friends while I was there. I'll make you a pot of her jambalaya while you're here."

She turned to Arnold. "You'll have to come try it, too! I promise it's the best thing you'll ever taste!"

"I don't doubt that," he answered with a small smile.

"What about the men?" Tommy teased. "Are you going to sit there and pretend you didn't find anyone worth mentioning?" He glanced at Arnold and winked. "My baby sister has always been a head-turner. I had to fight guys off like crazy in high school."

"There were a few," she admitted, her lips twisting into a shy grin. "A talented jazz drummer…an artist who taught me the proper way to use a paintbrush…a literature professor." Her cheeks burned. "It's certainly nothing I want to talk to my big brother about."

"Have you ever been in love?" Arnold blurted.

Heat pinched Twila's cheeks as she closed her eyes and remembered each of her lovers. She clearly recalled the times she'd shared a chair with the drummer as he taught her how to properly handle a drumstick, and all the festivals they'd attended while she was encased in his arms. Her heart swelled when she recalled how the artist looked at her when she volunteered to let him paint her nude. Her lips stretched with a glowing smile when remembering the late nights star-gazing with the professor as he read her poetry. She'd been in love with every single one of them.

They had all been a passionate kind of love, burning bright in the short time they lasted. None of their relationships had the stamina to last forever. She wasn't sure that was something she wanted anyway. She thrived on the heart-stopping thrill that came with every new relationship and the buzz that consumed her body the first time their lips touched. She was convinced the excitement of getting to know a man she liked carried over into her paintings.

"As a matter of fact, I have," she finally answered Arnold. "Have you?"

"I don't think so," he admitted with a slight pink color rising in the apples of his cheeks.

What a shame, Twila thought to herself.

"Does that mean you're a virgin?" Tommy asked him.

"Tommy!" Twila snapped. "Don't be so rude!"

Just then, a flurry of wild knocks fell at the front door. Chuckling at his sister's scolding, Tommy jumped to his feet and quickly answered, finding a handful of his high school buddies ready to greet him with hugs, weed, and several 6-packs of beer.

"Looks like we're in for a late night," Twila told Arnold a moment before the other men rushed inside to sweep her off her feet in greeting.

Arnold kept to himself for the rest of the night, sipping beer in one of the plastic camping chairs beside the fire pit in their backyard. Twila got caught up in stories of old times with her brother's friends. She'd spent considerable time with Tommy and his friends as they had only been a grade above her in the small Papaya Springs high school. As much as they flirted with Twila, she couldn't take her eyes off Arnold the entire night.

There was something mysteriously enduring about the man. How was it that someone so handsome had never experienced love? She sensed it was due in part to his shyness. He hadn't tried to interact with Tommy or his friends and seemed content to be sitting alone.

Finally, once the neighborhood became blanketed with darkness, she forced herself to break free of the reminiscing tales and check in on him.

"Sorry," she began as she approached him and fell into the open chair at his side. "I didn't mean to ignore you. I just haven't seen those guys in over four years. We hung out a lot when they were seniors." She eyed his can of beer. "Need a refill?"

"Nah, I think I'll head in for the night." He bent to retrieve his crutches piled on the ground. Twila beat him to it, holding them out of his reach with a teasing smile.

"Will you stay up a little longer if I promise to sit with you?"

His brow bunched up. "Why would you want to do that?"

"Because I'd like to get to know you better."

He responded with a gruff laugh. "What's an

oaf like me have to offer a beautiful woman like you?"

"You have a very striking face," she blurted. "One that I don't think I could forget if I tried." All at once, feeling shy, she dipped her chin. "Would you be interested in posing for me sometime? I'd love to attempt to capture it on a canvas."

Anger slipped over his features. "If this is some kind of joke——"

"It's not," she promised, setting the crutches back onto the ground by her feet. She took one of his hands with hers, feeling an overwhelming thrill when their skin touched and her hand disappeared inside his large grip. She lived for that sensation and wanted more. Her heart beat a little faster when she looked into his eyes. "You're very handsome, Arnold. And you seem sweet. In fact, if you asked me to go out on a date with you, I'd probably say 'yes'."

His eyes sparked with a gleam of hope against the darkness. "*Probably*?"

"Okay, *definitely*," she amended, lacing their fingers together. The buzz from their connected skin warmed her belly.

"I don't have a lot of money right now," he admitted, his lips pulling into a frown. "The disability checks will take a while to start coming in, and I don't know how long it'll be before I can work again."

She squeezed his hand. "That's okay. Money doesn't impress me anyway. We could go for a picnic on the beach tomorrow after we've spent some time working on your apartment."

"That sounds nice," he decided, squeezing her hand back. "I'd like that."

Twila's smile grew. "Me too."

As they dove deep into conversation, hands still held, Twila caught Tommy glaring at them from across the yard. Since Arnold was staring into the fire as he spoke, Twila stuck her tongue out at her brother. She wouldn't let anyone tell her who she could or couldn't date.

CHAPTER ELEVEN

Twila's first picnic on the beach with Arnie—as he preferred to be called—was everything she'd hoped for. He was still a bit withdrawn around her, so she had been the one to initiate their first kiss. The way he gently cradled her head and kissed her back with some hesitation made her wonder if Tommy was right—if Arnie was still a virgin.

That picnic evolved into more dates, leading to more hand holding and, eventually, endless passion. Before long, Twila found herself once again in love.

For several weeks, Twila and Arnie spent nearly every waking moment together. She sewed curtains for the window and a new divider for his bathroom. She planted a community garden behind the apartment building, providing fresh fruits and vegetables to share with the other tenants. When Arnie found a couch on the side of the road that was in halfway decent condition, she sewed a slip-cover to go over it and bought pillows from the thrift store to liven it up.

By the time the two of them were done scrubbing and painting, Twila had to admit she was satisfied enough that even she wouldn't mind living there.

One day, she saw a mouse scurry across the floor. She scared Arnie when she jumped on one of the kitchen chairs and squealed in surprise.

"What in the hell is wrong with you, woman?" he scolded, gripping his chest. "You should know better than to surprise a man who's spent time in the jungle, fearing for his life!"

"I'm sorry!" she said with a little cry. "I saw a mouse!"

He shook his head, disappointed. "A little mouse isn't going to hurt you. I'll make a run to the hardware store and pick up some traps. He'll be dead by morning."

Twila leaped off the chair. "You can't kill him!" she pleaded, tugging on his arm. "He's just an innocent creature! I'll somehow catch him and set him free!"

"You think you can catch it with your bare hands?"

"I'll put some cheese in a bucket or something," she decided, tears filling her eyes. "I'll do whatever it takes. Just promise me you won't kill him!"

With a gentle laugh, he took her into his arms and dropped a kiss inside her hair. "From now on, I'll call you 'my little mouse.' It's the perfect nickname, considering our size difference and your kindness towards animals."

Tears stung her eyes when she grumbled in reply, "Then maybe I'll start calling you 'my big moose.'"

Although there were times Arnie was frustrated with his lack of progress in healing and displayed a deep-seated temper Twila had been unaware he possessed, he was nothing but kind and gentle with her. He was patient without fail as she honed in on her ability to adequately capture faces with oils, using him as a model countless times before she decided she had earned the right to be proud of her work.

He built her an easel that always remained upright by the window. After being hired by a local car parts factory, he occasionally bought her painting supplies. Although he wasn't the best cook, he ensured she didn't starve when she was too caught up in a painting to stop. He never complained when she asked him to pose or dragged him to local art festivals. He had become, in Twila's opinion, the perfect lover.

As time went by, Twila built up enough confidence to paint other faces from a mix of her memories and the small collection of Polaroids she'd collected on her adventures over the years. Her favorite, a close-up of Miss Penny from New Orleans, earned a place of honor on one of Arnie's apartment walls. It was her best work, but she didn't have the heart to sell it. She eventually sold several others to a local art studio, earning enough royalties to purchase a brand-new bed and refrigerator for Arnie's apartment since he refused to let her contribute toward rent.

By that point, she was living with him full-time. Although he hadn't officially asked her to move in with him, he had begged her to stay with him nearly every night, and she had started bringing over enough of her belongings that it simply progressed over time.

They'd been together for nearly a year when she began to grow restless. She hadn't planned on staying in Papaya Springs for so long, especially once Tommy decided to move into a house with a buddy in Los Angeles. Her friends in New Orleans had expected her to return shortly after she'd welcomed Tommy home. She often received a letter from one or more of them, begging her to return.

Arnie didn't have any friends, which Twila found odd and frustrating. She craved time alone or with friends, but Arnie was always at her side whenever he wasn't at work. It became suffocating. She repeatedly asked if he had met anyone interesting at the factory, and nearly every week, she encouraged him to invite someone over for dinner. Although she had never sensed Arnie's oddness her brother once spoke of, she wondered if it was only because Arnie loved her. She was beginning to suspect he didn't warm up to strangers.

Arnie also didn't like to travel. Accordingly, he refused every one of Twila's proposed road trips. He claimed it brought back too many tragic memories from Vietnam. She missed the adventures of discovering new places and became stir-crazy. Whenever she wanted to visit Tommy, she was forced to navigate through the harrowing streets of Lost Angeles on her own.

On one of her trips to the big city, Tommy took her to a music and art festival downtown. Twila felt most at home surrounded by other artists and immersed in that atmosphere. She stopped at nearly every booth, deciding it never hurt to network with like-minded individuals. As she met countless men and women with the potential to one day become her friends, she cursed herself for agreeing to settle down with Arnie.

Later in the afternoon, while her brother flirted with a belly dancer getting ready to take one of the stages, Twila met a man named Henry who owned an art studio in downtown Los Angeles. Henry was an attractive, willowy man with a thick mustache, curly dark hair, and kind, russet eyes. He was significantly older than Twila, possibly edging toward fifty. His rust-colored checkered shirt and white polyester pants were stylish enough for a disco floor, and he possessed a killer smile with deep dimples on either side. Twila was unquestionably drawn to his knowledge of art and ability to tell engaging stories of famous artists he'd met.

Her conversation with Henry continued effortlessly as they moved over to a booth run by a local distillery and indulged in locally-made brews. Between bouts of laughter, Twila realized she hadn't felt so carefree and elated since moving in with Arnie.

Once her mind began to buzz from the alcohol, she found herself wondering what her life would've been like if she had ignored the wounded soldier at the bus station. Would she have felt the tickle of Henry's mustache when they kissed? Would she have gone home with him that night and continued their conversation between lovemaking sessions? Would she have eventually relocated to Los Angeles, where the artist community thrived?

They became so engaged in conversation that Twila didn't notice when the sun set and the street lights glowed overhead. Until Tommy joined them, she had forgotten she had yet to drive back to Papaya Springs.

"Tommy!" she exclaimed, wrapping her arm around her brother's waist and knocking over an empty beer cup. "Henry, this is my big brother, Tommy!"

Henry tilted his chin in greeting. "Don't tell me you're here to steal your beautiful sister away from me, Tommy. She's a real delight." He reached across the picnic table to squeeze Twila's hand. "So well-educated in the art scene."

"She has a long drive ahead of her," Tommy scolded, glancing at the stack of remaining empty cups between them. "We need to get going."

Henry set his hand on Tommy's shoulder. "Nonsense, son. I own a large loft just down the street. You're both welcome to crash there for the night. You could join me at the disco next door if you're inclined."

"We'd hate to put you out like that," Twila told him.

Henry's mustache lifted above a broad smile. "It's no bother. I entertain guests frequently. It's an enjoyable pastime."

Tommy gave Twila a thoughtful glance as if wanting her to make the call. He hadn't been a fan of Arnie from the start, and she sensed he had also been instantly charmed by Henry.

"Do you need to return home for some reason?" she asked her brother, quirking one eyebrow as if silently asking, *"Why not?"*

He glanced over his shoulder, watching the belly dancer interact with a circle of friends. She caught Tommy's gaze and offered a little wave before giggling with her friends. "Actually, the disco sounds like a great idea," Tommy decided, licking his lips.

"Feel free to invite your little friend to join us," Henry told him. "I have enough party favors for everyone," he added, wiggling his thick eyebrows and grinning.

Tommy grinned back at him. "Groovy." He hurried back to the belly dancer with a smile almost splitting his cheeks.

A slight twinge of unease stirred through Twila as she considered their plan a little more. Arnie didn't have a telephone. It was an added expense he insisted they could do without. How would she tell him she wouldn't return until morning? She could only hope he would understand.

Besides, they weren't really committed to each other. It wasn't like Arnie *owned* her or anything. And spending time with Henry could lead to bigger things. After all, making the right connections often achieved success as an artist.

"Everything alright, love?" Henry asked, moving in closer.

Twila stared at his pale pink lips beneath the impressive mustache. She had never been with a man over forty. If she decided to be with him, she could break things off with Arnie the next day and let him know she found someone else she wanted to be with.

Still, as many times as she fell in and out of love, she had never "cheated" on anyone. She decided it would be unfair to both Arnie *and* Henry if she were to act on her feelings.

"I'm with someone," she admitted with a guilt-ridden grimace. "Another man. We live together. I'm sorry if I unfairly led you on. Maybe in another life—"

"Good *heavens!*" Henry choked on a bout of laughter. "I didn't stop to think how my proposal must sound! Dear girl, I'm happily married. I merely enjoyed your company today and wish to nurture this new friendship. My wife is already at the disco, and I was hoping to introduce you to each other. The studio apartment is something we occasionally use to entertain guests…my wife and I won't be staying there along with you." His cheeks turned a dark shade of red. "I will admit I thought you would be a perfect match for my boy, Thomas, but clearly, that's off the table. I would, however, be pleased if you would stop by the studio in the morning and perhaps demonstrate your method to my wife. She's actively searching for an artist who specializes in oil paintings to feature at her next exhibit."

Embarrassment scorched Twila's face. "I'm so sorry. I should never have assumed—"

Henry patted her hand once more and winked. "Perhaps in another life."

Humiliation continued swelled through Twila as

they watched Tommy and the belly dancer approach. Her brother's arm was slung around the woman's neck in an overly friendly way, making Twila wonder if he had already snuck off with the woman earlier to fool around. Part of her wanted to pull her brother aside and beg him to take her back to his place for the night. Although she had too much to drink to get behind the wheel, Tommy seemed sober.

Nonetheless, they danced at the disco until the wee hours of the morning with Henry, his wife, and the artsy couple's friends. Deciding she'd had the time of her life, Twila instantly passed out on the luxurious leather couch in Henry's loft.

She could not know her little adventure had awakened a dormant beast.

CHAPTER TWELVE

Arnie was sitting at the kitchen table when Twila returned from her trip to Los Angeles early the following day. The way he sat rigid, his cold stare boring into her soul, she realized she had made a terrible mistake by not coming home the night before. The dark intent he omitted made her skin crawl and her insides tighten.

She quickly decided it would be best to make light of the situation and pretend nothing was amiss. "Arnie!" she sang, breezing into the apartment to kiss his cheek. "Why aren't you at work?"

"Where have you been?" he demanded in a low growl. "I was afraid you had died in a car accident."

"Clearly, I'm fine," she said, backing away with

a nervous giggle. "I merely had too much to drink with Tommy at an art festival. I spent the night on his couch. If you had a telephone, I would have called to let you know." As much as she strived to be transparent with her lovers, she was confident Arnie wouldn't understand the platonic friendship she'd formed with Henry.

"I was on the verge of making a trip to the police station," he informed her, baring his teeth in an angry sneer. He grabbed his cane, wavering as he stood. "How could you have done something so cruel to me, Little Mouse?" As he shuffled closer, his expression darkened. "I trusted you."

Her voice wavered with fear when she said, "I'm so sorry I scared you like that. Truly."

"I thought you loved me."

"I do!" she cried, holding onto his fierce face. "I didn't mean to hurt you, Arnie. It's just…I haven't spent time with other artists in ages. Being around them was so enlightening. It was good for my soul."

He remained as hard as marble beneath her touch. "And I'm not?"

"Of course you are!" she insisted. "Just in different ways."

The hard look in his gaze didn't falter as he walked away from her to exit the apartment.

The next afternoon, she received a letter from New Orleans that nearly broke her heart. To make things worse, Arnie returned from work in a sour mood. The moment he opened the door to the apartment, he chucked his cane across the room. It shattered a vase full of flowers he'd given her that sat in the center of their 2-person kitchen table. Twila's heart slammed to a stop in her chest. He had gone to work after their argument the day before and hadn't spoken to her since.

"Is everything okay?" she asked meekly while wiping her swollen eyes.

"Got fired today," he grunted. With one look at her distressed state, he fell to his knees and buried his head inside her lap. "I'm so sorry, my little mouse! I'll never be able to provide for you properly as long as I'm a cripple!" His fingers gripped her skirt as he began to cry. "What kind of man can't take care of the woman he loves? I'll never be able to buy you a wedding ring at this rate!"

Twila's breaths became thin. In the time they'd been together, they had never once discussed marriage. Although he had expressed an interest in starting a family one day, she assumed he meant with a woman sometime in the future and not necessarily with *her*.

Promising herself to one man until the end of time made her stomach harden. Without the rush of falling in love for the first time with someone, she wasn't sure her creativity would continue to flourish. She also didn't think she'd ever enjoy staying in one place for long, and Arnie didn't enjoy traveling outside Papaya Springs.

"There's no need to be upset," she cooed, running her fingers through the thick, sandy hair he'd grown down to his chin. "I will still love you, no matter what."

With the scratchy sound of her voice, he lifted his head to look her in the eye. "You've been crying. What's wrong?"

Twila's lips quivered. "I received a letter from Miss Penny's son today. She passed away last week."

With a frown, Arnie gazed at the portrait above Twila's head. "She was old, Little Mouse. Old people die."

"It doesn't matter," Twila told him with a shake of her head. "She was a very dear friend. I should've been there to say goodbye." She gripped his arms, pulling him upright. "I have to go to her funeral, Arnie. It's on Sunday…in New Orleans.

Two days isn't enough time to drive out there. I'll have to fly."

The same dark, unsettling look from their last argument stirred behind his eyes. "I can't afford to fly you to New Orleans."

"I still have a big chunk of money in the bank from selling my paintings," she explained. "I can afford to pay for my own flight."

"You'd go without me?" he snarled.

She bit her bottom lip. As much as he disliked flying after returning from 'Nam, she assumed he wouldn't want to go. "I suppose I could afford to buy you a ticket as well. But things might be a little tight for a while after that. At least until I can sell some more paintings."

She craned her neck to look up at Miss Penny's likeness. She didn't think she had the heart to sell the painting now that her friend was gone, but if Arnie didn't find another job soon…

"Go ahead without me then," he grumbled, hobbling back to his feet. "It's silly to spend that kind of money on someone who won't know whether or not you were there to begin with."

In that tense moment, Twila knew she had to find a way out of their relationship. Arnold Douglas was no longer the man she'd met at the bus station.

The summertime humidity in New Orleans was brutal. Twila fanned herself alongside Miss Penny's daughter-in-law as the procession wound through the city's neighborhood streets. Sweat dripped down her back and face, mingling with her endless tears.

Twila had seen countless jazz funerals when she'd lived there, but never attended one for a friend. The brass wail of trumpets and trombones and the drums' resounding thuds added to her sorrow and lifted her spirits in a complicated way she couldn't explain. Miss Penny's grandchildren were a collective representation of the spirited way the sweet woman had lived as most of them wept with smiles and a little swing to their hips. Miss Penny's three great-grandchildren joyously danced among them, their little hands flashing and waving to the sorrowful beat. Twila's fingers itched to capture the precious memory in a painting.

She'd been delighted to discover Walter, her one-time lover, was the drummer in the procession. She had hoped he would be there since he was Miss Penny's neighbor and had introduced Twila to the kindly old woman. As soon as Miss Penny's celebration concluded, they ran to each other with a firm embrace. Twila melted to the ground with the familiar feeling of his strong arms and lithe body.

"What ails you, Miss Twila?" he asked as they parted, his eyes glowing with concern against his dark skin. "I don't think I've ever seen you look this down, and I sense it's not only because of Miss Penny's passin'."

All at once, her spirit felt utterly drained. Arnie had refused to speak to her after she returned from the travel agency with her ticket. She dreaded returning to him and letting him know they were done.

"I'm sure Miss Penny told you I stayed in California," she reluctantly explained to Walter. "That wasn't part of my plan, but I sort of…umm…"

"Fell in love," he supplied with a grin. "Miss Penny told me all about it. Said you got that big heart of yours stolen by a wounded soldier."

"Arnie's a good man, for the most part. It's just…"

"You've got the soul of an exotic bird." His gaze became gentle as he tucked a wayward strand of hair behind her ear. "Too beautiful to be caged up somewhere for one man to admire." His beautiful smile widened. "Lord knows I tried."

Fresh tears sprang to her eyes. Perhaps she had

been too hasty to walk away from Walter after he'd proposed they elope with the aid of a minister at the next jazz festival. He seemed to know her better than anyone, and the affectionate way he was looking at her, she knew he still loved her. Deeply.

"I'd been workin' up the courage to get your phone number from Miss Penny," he confessed with a shy grin. "My sister, Rosalyn, recently decided to study art abroad…she's leavin' next month. When she broke the news, she said it was too bad you weren't still around, or she would've invited you to come along as a freeloadin' roommate. I told her there was nothin' stoppin' her from askin' even though you'd moved on. But she didn't think you'd be interested."

Pangs of jealousy stole Twila's breath. Walter's parents owned a successful jazz club in the French Quarter and had become quite wealthy when Walter and his sister were young. When Rosalyn mentioned "freeloading," it was because she knew Twila couldn't afford such an elaborate trip. The two women had become close in the eighteen months Twila and Walter had been together, so Twila was confident Rosalyn's invitation had been genuine.

"Where's she going?" Twila asked in a quiet voice.

"Paris, London, Santorini, Rome, and a handful of other places I don't remember because I've never heard of 'em." With a deep chuckle, he waved his hands through the air. "Of course, our folks supported the idea of you comin' along because they knew you'd make sure their Rosie behaved herself."

Twila briefly allowed herself to imagine traveling the world at her old friend's side and witnessing first-hand some of the most famous works of art known to man. Ever since she was a little girl, she dreamed of walking inside the Sistine Chapel and drinking in Michelangelo's masterpiece with her own eyes. She would surely faint if she were to stand in front of da Vinci's Mona Lisa or Van Gogh's Self-Portrait.

More tears spilled down her cheeks as she imagined her wildest dreams coming to fruition. She knew it would break Arnie's tender heart if she accepted the invitation to join her friend, but it was also a way out. If she stayed in California only to make him happy, a small part of her would shrivel up and die. She refused to become a shell of her former self like her mother.

Walter had become little more than a blur through her tears. "Do you think she'd still…I mean, did she really mean to invite me to come along? Was she serious when she said that?"

"I can take you to see her right now so she can ask you face-to-face. She's workin' at the club. She'd be overjoyed to see your pretty face—especially if you mean to take her up on the invitation."

Sniffling, Twila wiped an arm across her wet face. "Do you think I should?"

"Baby girl," Walter whispered, pulling her back into his arms, "I believe it's exactly the kind of adventure that exotic soul of yours craves."

CHAPTER THIRTEEN

Twila's legs felt impossibly heavy as she climbed the rickety steps to Arnie's apartment early in the evening following Miss Penny's funeral. On the return flight from Louisiana, she tried to imagine the best way to tell Arnie that she had decided to leave. Considering his comment about marriage the other day, she suspected he'd be devastated no matter how she chose to break the news. One thing was sure—she wouldn't dare mention her former lover's influence on her decision.

She was worried Arnie had forgotten to pay the electric bill when she swung the door open to find the apartment illuminated by multiple candles. Then she noticed him waiting on one of the two kitchen chairs, a small velvet box on the table before him. Stifling a sharp gasp, she quickly covered her mouth with one hand and dropped her suitcase with the other.

So much for letting him down easily.

"Arnie…" she began, too surprised to go on.

He rushed over to her as fast as his wounded leg would allow and guided her toward the other chair. She was in such an advanced state of shock that she feared she would've fallen over without his help. It was as if she had been transported into a nightmare.

"I'm sorry, my little mouse. I was so…so *angry* when you left for your friend's funeral that I wasn't thinking straight. It's just…I knew you had many other lovers before me. I was afraid you were secretly returning to New Orleans so you could be reunited with one. I was worried I wasn't enough for you anymore."

With great difficulty, he lowered to his good knee and tried to physically crook the other leg in front of him with both hands. The way he grimaced and grunted was enough to drive Twila insane with guilt.

"Arnie, stop," she pleaded, resting her hand on his shoulder. "We have to talk."

"What do you think I'm trying to do here?" he snapped, casting her one of his dangerous looks.

"It looks like you're attempting to ask for my hand in marriage, and that's not where the conversation I want to have with you will be headed."

"What is *that* supposed to mean?"

Her stomach tightened. His voice was strained with more anger every time he spoke. "Why don't you take a seat? You look…uncomfortable."

"Don't be telling me what to do," he growled, even though he was clearly trying to rise from the floor.

She tried to steady him by gripping his forearms, but he jerked away and tumbled onto his back. Wincing, she reached for him a second time. "Arnie—"

"Get away from me!" he roared.

In the time it took for him to recover and get back on his feet, she looked away. Watching him without helping felt heartless and cruel. She merely wished for the whole ordeal to end so she could peacefully mourn their relationship.

She'd never had to experience an ugly argument when leaving men in the past. Except for Walter, the others had understood their time together was temporary. And although Walter had once believed they were soul mates, he'd been gracious when she told him it was time for her to move on.

She wasn't sure she had the heart to continue hurting Arnold that way.

He finally lowered to the chair across from her and screwed his eyelids shut. "What are you saying? Are you breaking up with me?"

As she eyed the box still sitting in front of him, her nerves buzzed with unease. Her timing couldn't be any worse. "You're a sweet man, Arnie. And I hope you understand how much I love you…I truly do. There will always be a piece of you in my heart."

"But there's a condition to that love?" he sneered, his eyes popping open.

Her heart temporarily stopped with the darkness coursing through his words.

"The kind of domesticated life you want is not for me," she explained, trying her best not to feed his anger. "I was meant to wander and explore the world. There's simply too much out there waiting to be discovered." She paused with a weak smile. "The idea of staying in one place for very long makes it hard for me to breathe."

His jaw hardened. "Then I'll go with you."

She reached for his hand, then thought better of it. "It's something I must do on my own, Arnie."

The darkness emitting from his eyes made Twila shudder. "You think your silly paintings will support you as you 'wander' the earth?"

The question felt like a slap in her face. Before that moment, he'd been so supportive of her work, referring to them as her "masterpieces."

She drew her gaze away from his. "I was offered a once-in-a-lifetime opportunity by a friend. I'd have the chance to study some of the greatest paintings in history and learn from world-renowned artists—"

"So I was right. You're leaving me for an old lover. This so-called *friend*."

"I'm not leaving you for anyone. This friend is a *woman*." She put her trembling hands in her lap, wishing her brother was beside her. Even more so, she wished she had taken Tommy's advice and stayed far away from Arnold Douglas as he had first suggested at the bus station.

"Look," she said, eyeing her soon-to-be ex-lover with growing trepidation, "it was never my intention to hurt you. My decision to go overseas has nothing to do with you or our relationship. I had fun with you, Arnie. It's just—"

"I'm not enough." His lips trembled with anger. "Say it, Twila. I'm not enough of a man for you."

"That's not true." Panic clenched her throat when she noticed his hands had balled into fists at his side. No matter what she said, he didn't seem to understand what she was trying to tell him. Explaining herself any more seemed futile. She rose on wobbling legs, feeling an urgent need to leave the little apartment far behind. "I think it's best to stay at my mother's tonight. I'll return tomorrow to get my things."

Arnold remained silent as she snatched her suitcase and hurried out the door.

———

After Twila called Tommy from a gas station phone booth to fill him in on her situation, he insisted on driving up from Los Angeles the following day to help her collect her things. She felt as if she was holding her breath the entire ride from their mother's house to the apartment, waiting for the inevitable "I told you so" speech that she was sure would be coming. But Tommy remained unusually quiet as he drove through the seedy neighborhood and parked in front of the building.

They planned their trip so they would arrive several hours after Arnie was to begin his shift at the factory. Even with Tommy at her side, she didn't want to face another confrontation when she packed her belongings.

Tommy gave the building a forlorn look. "It breaks my heart to think you called this dump home for so long."

"It wasn't so bad. Arnie and I made some good memories here."

He turned to her, draping an arm on the seat behind her. "I never understood what you saw in that guy. Sometimes, I thought maybe it was because he was hurt and needed help."

"It was more than that," she muttered, glancing at the second story. "At least in the beginning."

With a slow exhale, Tommy removed the keys from the ignition and jingled them inside his hand. "You know what I think, sis? Even though I'll miss you like crazy, your plan to leave the country is the best idea you've ever had."

With a burst of delight, she sat up a little taller. Besides Arnie, Walter, and his sister, Tommy was the only one who knew she was leaving. She'd laid awake in her childhood bed most of the night, worried she was making a mistake. "You think so?"

He gave an affirmative hum. "You've never understood how special you are. You should take this time away to really think about what you want out of life and try not to get caught up in worrying about others. You don't realize it's not up to you to save every less fortunate person you meet. Now, I'm not saying you should remain celibate while you're over there. I just want you to step back and understand you're too good to fall in love with just anyone. You should wait next time until you find someone worthy of you."

Beaming, she leaned over to kiss her brother's cheek. "I love you, Tommy. Sometimes you sound a little crazy, but I love you all the same."

"Love you too, sis." He jerked his chin at the building. "Let's hurry up and get this over with. I wanna try that new taco stand we passed on the way here."

Tommy led the way up to the apartment, repeatedly sweeping his eyes around them as if waiting for an ambush.

As soon as Twila unlocked the door, she sensed something was amiss. A funny premonition lingered in her chest as she breathed in the stale summer air breezing through the apartment's sole window.

"What's wrong?" Tommy asked.

"I'm not—"

Then she saw it.

Her beloved painting of Miss Penny had been ripped to shreds. From the sharp lines left behind, Twila presumed a knife had been used to desecrate the canvas.

Mouth ajar, she dropped down onto the couch.

"Oh, god," she whispered as her mind raced to understand what had happened. *Had one of the bums who squatted inside the old buildings nearby broken into their home?*

Eyes watering, she scanned the rest of the small space, almost *praying* to find signs of a break-in. She couldn't imagine her Arnie would be responsible for such a deplorable act, but the rest of the apartment appeared in its normal condition.

Until she spotted the bowl filled with her precious Polaroids.

They, too, had been ripped to shreds.

"That psycho!" Tommy exclaimed, shouldering past her to point at her miniature studio beneath the window. "I'll kill him!"

When she stepped in behind her brother, she saw her art supplies had also been destroyed. The easel Arnie had built lay in a pile of scraps. The two canvases she'd been working on were smeared with various oil paint colors, and the empty tubes had been discarded on the floor.

"Hurry up and get your things packed," Tommy told her, forming fists at his sides. "Then you're coming to L.A. with me until you leave for Europe. I won't let this lunatic anywhere near you again."

Twila's heart pounded furiously as she stuffed her remaining belongings into her battered suitcase, leaving behind her destroyed artwork and memories.

She couldn't leave Papaya Springs soon enough.

PART III

CHAPTER FOURTEEN
PAPAYA SPRINGS, CALIFORNIA

APRIL 9TH

With the conclusion of Twila's story, Bexley set her right hand over Twila's. "You told me your relationships all ended amicably."

"My brain must've done everything in its power to cast those ugly memories of Arnold aside," Twila decided, blinking back tears. "I haven't thought about that day in forever."

"It's called self-preservation," Brewer said to her, his expression oozing with kindness. "Happens to the best of us."

An unexpected wave of sadness swept through Bexley as she recalled some of the ugly memories her husband had cast aside. She gently rubbed the back of her elderly friend's hand. "I can't believe he destroyed that painting of your friend. At the same time, it's not too far of a stretch to imagine someone with that kind of anger evolving into a killer."

Twila swiped her tears with the back of her free hand. "You really think he killed that woman?"

"I think it's likely," Bexley answered, "especially when considering his nickname for you and the note left at the scene."

Brewer reached behind him to grab a box of tissues from the counter and set them on the table in front of Twila. "I agree with Bex. We need to fill Deputy Danks in on this Arnold guy and request they keep a squad car parked outside your house until they locate his whereabouts."

Bexley gently squeezed her friend's hand. "I know you aren't going to like this, but it's time to call J.J., too. He'll skin me alive if he gets word of this from another source." When Twila opened her mouth to protest, Bexley gave a terse shake of her head. "He'd never forgive himself if something were to happen, and he wasn't here to protect you, Twila."

Twila sighed heavily as she removed a tissue from the box and patted her eyes. "I suppose you're right."

Out of the blue, Bexley's last bite of tuna casserole rose inside her stomach and climbed up her esophagus. She excused herself with hardly a minute to spare before losing her lunch inside the toilet bowl of Twila's guest bathroom. Once done, she rinsed her mouth with water and gazed back at her reflection over the sink. She looked every bit as tired as she felt.

Grasping onto the edges of the porcelain sink, her mind raced as she tried to remember the last time she'd had a period. She remembered having one a month or so after Easton was born because she'd joked to Brewer that night that her body had reminded her by menstruating a few days early. But after that…she came up with nothing. She'd been taking her pills religiously. How could she be pregnant?

"Oh, my god," she muttered. "This can't be happening."

Another bout of nausea forced her to kneel down in front of the toilet a second time.

Late Monday morning, as Bexley pulled up to the gate in front of Carla and Diego Garcia's residence, she willed her pulse to become steady. While it had only taken Red a handful of minutes to locate the address for Tabitha's sister, it was dumb luck that Carla Garcia had recently posted a search for a nanny on social media.

Still, Bexley's anxious mood went far beyond Jack's situation. It had been a painfully long night, even with J.J. and a deputy watching over Twila. In addition to worrying about her friend's safety, she dreaded having to tell Brewer that she may be carrying a rugrat that neither of them wanted.

"One crisis at a time," Bexley muttered, squeezing her eyes shut.

"May I help you?" a sultry female voice called over the intercom at her side.

Bexley leaned out her window to speak into the metal box. "I'm here to meet with Carla Garcia."

"Who are you?"

"My name is Bexley Hawkins." As there was no way of knowing whether Tabitha would've mentioned Bexley's name to her sister, she decided her married name was the safest bet. "I'm here about the nanny position."

"I don't see your name on the list."

Bexley's hands tightened on her steering wheel. "Check again. I'm the woman Temperance Rose called to recommend earlier this morning."

There was a hesitation before the voice replied, "Oh, right. Come on in, Miss Hawkins. You can park right in front of the house."

As Bexley rolled through the open gates, she made a mental note to do something special for Temperance. She already owed her friend a mountain of favors and had felt guilty about asking for another one. At least when Bexley called, the former reality star had already been awake, making breakfast for Olive before she left for school.

While Bexley recognized the neighborhood, she hadn't been expecting to find a dwelling merely a step or two down from that of Carla's famous news anchor sister. After all, Diego Garcia's online resume revealed a history of positions in fast food management, and Carla's last known job involved customer service. The 2-story stucco monstrosity with a red terracotta roof and arched windows was not something an average office manager could afford.

A curvy, middle-aged woman with unremarkable features answered the door. Although Carla had the same sharp eyes and dark hair as her sister, the skin from the woman's mouth down to her chin was pulled unnaturally tight from either Botox or surgery. In a revealing 2-piece swimsuit with a mesh coverup draped over her shoulders and oversized sunglasses perched on top of her head, it was apparent Bexley had interrupted a leisurely morning.

Bexley flashed a cheerleader-worthy smile. "It's nice to meet you, Mrs. Garcia. I'm Bexley."

The woman shook Bexley's hand before ushering her inside. "Please, call me Carla."

"Your home is beautiful," Bexley commented, trailing behind as the woman headed farther into the house. The house was elaborately designed with dark wood beams and high-end furniture the same shade of off-white as the carpet. Bexley couldn't begin to imagine what it must've been like for a child to live in such a pristine environment.

The woman *tsked*. "I'm sure it's not half as impressive as Temperance Rose's estate."

"You got me there," Bexley admitted.

As they passed through a grand sitting area flanked by gaudy water fountains, a family portrait caught Bexley's attention. Sitting between Carla and a round-faced man, a handsome boy around ten beamed at the camera.

The same boy Tabitha had picked up from the gym.

On closer inspection, the boy possessed Tabitha's dark eyes, and his skin was darker than most Caucasians could get from a healthy tan. His Anglo-Saxon nose and lips shared nearly identical angles to those of Jack's as a child. Most telling, his flaxen hair, grown past his ears in a trendy style often seen on young boys, appeared natural as there wasn't the slightest bit of darkness at his roots.

"Is that your son?" Bexley asked.

The woman regarded the portrait with a hesitant smile that spoke volumes. "That's our Johnny."

Bexley suppressed the urge to yell at the woman. *That was Jack's father's name.* "He's adorable," she said, forcing herself to smile. "I bet he'd look great in front of a T.V. camera. I understand that career path is common in his family—on both sides."

Carla whirled on her, crossing her arms beneath her chest. "Are you a reporter?" she spat with an accusatory glare.

"I'm a private investigator," Bexley admitted, mirroring the woman's body language. "I'm here because I know that boy's parents are your sister and Jack Squires."

"W-what?" Mouth agape, Carla dropped down onto the couch. She stared straight ahead, chest heaving with panicked breaths. "You don't—I can't—"

"Deep breaths, Mrs. Garcia. Don't make me call an ambulance." Bexley shuffled closer. "I'm here to discover why you're raising Tabitha's son without telling his father of his existence and what made your husband flip out on your sister."

Carla's eyes filled with tears as she met Bexley's gaze. "Who told you?"

"I saw Tabitha with little Johnny the other day. With a few minor exceptions, he's a clone of his father at that age." Mustering the slow, gentle tone Cineste teasingly referred to as her "teacher's voice," Bexley perched on the couch at the woman's side. "Listen, Mrs. Garcia. I'm not going to tell anyone your secret. I'm here because your sister filed a bogus claim against Jack, that boy's father, and he'd very much like to see it dropped. Jack is also interested in having a relationship with his son."

"Everything spiraled out of control so quickly," Carla admitted among more tears. "My sister and I were once very close—it's the only reason I volunteered to take Johnny in as my own. She didn't want the burden of a child, and she didn't want the public to judge her for giving him away. I loved him long before he came into this world. I couldn't let him live with some stranger. He was family! Our arrangement worked out perfectly because my husband and I could not have children of our own. Then Diego lost his job and got it in his thick head to extort money from Tabby."

"And that's when the police got involved," Bexley assumed. "He hadn't merely lost his mind, as she suggested in her interviews. He was demanding money."

"I tried to talk him out of it. I didn't want to do that to my sister! She was already kind enough to help with the expenses we incurred from raising Johnny. Then Diego threatened her with a gun, and I called the police. I never imagined the situation would lead to Diego serving time in prison."

Bexley slowly shook her head as if she agreed such an illegal action shouldn't lead to any serious consequences. She would do anything to encourage the woman to continue.

"Diego made me swear I would never reveal our secret to anyone. I have…until now. It's just…I'm so *tired*. Being a single mom to such an active boy is more work than I imagined. I begged Tabby to help me out…to step up a little in her role as his aunt. She's been giving him a ride here and there to his activities but claims she's too busy to do anything more. That's why I'm looking to hire a nanny."

Maybe you should ask his birth father to help out, Bexley thought, finding it extremely difficult not to utter the words aloud. "Why did Tabitha wait this long to go after Jack for money?"

"With every day Diego has spent behind bars, he's become more and more delusional. He thinks Tabby should reward him for going to prison. He claims she wouldn't have become rich and famous if he hadn't threatened her with that kind of force. She finally gave in and sent large sums of cash—enough to rent this place. But that still wasn't enough for Diego. He said he'd tell Jack Squires her secret if she didn't hand over five million. She tried to tell him she doesn't have that much equity, but he wouldn't listen." More tears spilled down her cheeks. "I don't want her money! I don't need a house this big! I just want my friendship with my sister back!"

Bexley wasn't sure how anyone could possibly untangle the mess Tabitha had created. As far as she was concerned, she had completed the job Jack had asked of her. It would be up to him to decide what to do next.

Giving the woman a barely masked look of disgust, Bexley stood. "I'm sure Jack's lawyer will be in touch."

CHAPTER FIFTEEN

Tears filled Jack's eyes as Bexley told him everything she had learned from Carla Garcia earlier that morning. "I can't believe it," he whispered. "I have a son." His lips bent with a little smirk. "I'm *a dad*."

Bexley grabbed his arm as he started to lower. He was a foot away from the makeup chair he'd been sitting in when she'd arrived at the station. "Easy, big guy," she said, guiding him to the proper spot. "Don't want that pretty face all banged up when you go on air."

"What now?" Jack asked, sounding completely overwhelmed. He ran his fingers through his perfectly styled hair. "Do I go to their house and demand to see him?"

"I'd suggest you start by calling your lawyer," Bexley answered truthfully. "Tabitha's sister may be overwhelmed and ready to accept help, but I sense she won't hand Johnny over without a fight. They've raised him as their son."

"Johnny," Jack repeated with another little grin as a tear slipped down his cheek. "I can't believe they named him after my father."

Bexley handed him a tissue from the makeup table. "I guess Tabitha did her research."

As Jack patted the moisture from around his eyes, Bexley's phone buzzed inside her pocket. She held a finger up to him before she stepped away.

"Bexley Squires."

"She took Johnny!" a woman's voice cried.

Bexley paused to place the voice. "Mrs. Garcia?"

"She must know about our conversation! I don't know how, but—oh god, she must have the house bugged!"

Bexley put more distance between herself and Jack, worried he'd overhear the conversation. "Take it easy, Carla. Let's start from the beginning. You think Tabitha took Johnny?"

"I *know* she did! I drove to the school to pick him up like always, but he wasn't there! I spoke to one of the aids the school hired to keep an eye on the kids after school lets out, and she said my sister came to get him, said something to Johnny about going for his first ride on a private jet!" The woman began to sob loudly. "Why's she doing this…to me? How could she…give him to me…then take him away again?"

"Carla," Bexley warned, "you need to calm down. I can't help if you're hysterical."

Carla exhaled stutteringly, then sniffled. "You're right…I'm sorry."

"Does your sister have access to a private jet?"

"She goes through a broker—always flies out of the PS private airport."

Bexley glanced back to where Jack grinned at his reflection in the mirror, surrounded by dozens of lightbulbs. She hated to burst his bubble, but it seemed necessary given the situation.

"Thanks for calling me," she told the woman. "This time, you did the right thing."

Jack's Tesla zipped in and out of traffic so quickly that it felt like the other cars weren't moving. Bexley felt the blood drain from her head as she gripped her seatbelt. "You aren't going to help the situation with your son if he meets you for the first time as a mangled piece of flesh inside a casket."

"If Tabitha gets on a private jet with him, I'll never see him again anyway!" Jack snapped. His strained gaze briefly met hers. "She has the means to disappear, Bex!"

"I understand the urgency, Jack. I really do." She braced her foot against the dashboard as he cut off a large tanker. "But if you don't calm the hell down before we get there, security will see you as a threat and take us both out. Then Tabitha would definitely win. I think it would be best if I approached her alone."

Jack shook his head repeatedly. "If I had manned up back when I first thought Tabitha was pregnant, if I had simply *asked her* if she was carrying my child, none of this would be happening. It's my fault for backing down in the first place. I need to confront her head-on. I won't stand by and let her take Johnny away from me a second time. Not when I've finally just discovered he exists."

When the Papaya Springs private airport entrance came into view, Bexley's muscles unclenched. She let out a shaking breath. "Fine. But you're going to have to get your shit together, Jack. Our chances of getting through the gates and onto the tarmac are already slim to none, considering we haven't heard back from Temperance."

Bexley cringed as she uttered her friend's name yet again. It was becoming painfully clear that she'd only be able to repay her friend by offering up one of Bexley's vital organs. When the call she placed to Temperance had kicked into voicemail, Bexley left a short, discombobulated message that involved the mere mention of Jack needing a massive favor for reasons she couldn't get into. Since Temperance and Jack were tentatively seeing each other, Bexley hadn't felt it was her place to fill Temperance in on Jack's situation with his estranged son.

After the security guard motioned them to continue past the gate with the mere mention of Temperance's name and the access they were granted to her jet, Jack raised his hand for Bexley to slap.

"Your date with her yesterday must've gone *extremely* well," she teased as their hands connected. "You should probably fill me in on the juicy details." She snuggled in a little closer to him, batting her eyelashes. "Did she giggle at all your dad jokes? Did your hands accidentally touch when you were reaching for something simultaneously? Did you share a plate of spaghetti?"

"I don't know how Brewer puts up with you," he teased back, rolling his eyes even though his lips bent with a grin.

Bexley pointed to the side of the runway. "There's a jet with the boarding stairs still out! I bet that's her!"

Jack accelerated in the direction she pointed, haphazardly parking at an angle alongside a small fleet of black cars and SUVs. He was out of the vehicle and on the move before Bexley could remind him to remain calm.

Bexley caught up to him at the base of the stairs, where he stood motionless, one hand gripping the railing. She was about to ask him what was wrong when she spotted little Johnny standing in the jet's open doorway, staring back at them. He was thin with bony cheeks and seemed taller than average to Bexley, even though she wasn't sure of the usual height for a 10-year-old. In a white t-shirt with the logo of Jack's favorite basketball team, black shorts, and white high tops, hair tousled like he'd just been running, there was no denying the kid was an adorable clone of the man staring back at him.

"H-hi," Jack stuttered, lifting a hand in a small wave.

The boy waved back with a little smile cracking his smooth lips.

"Where's your Aunt Tabitha?" Bexley asked him.

The infamous news anchor stepped in behind him with a deep scowl. "I'm right here."

"Tabitha," Jack said to her, his deep voice casting a clear warning, "it seems we're past due for an important conversation."

As Tabitha and Jack discussed their situation in the back of her private car, Bexley sat beside Johnny in one of the luxurious leather seats inside the small jet. The toy airplane the pilot gifted the boy sat in his lap, untouched. Johnny tapped his fingers against the armrests at his sides, clearly unsettled by what he had just witnessed. Bexley had become comfortable enough around Olive, but young boys were an entirely different creature.

"My name's Bexley," she said once the silence became stifling. "What's yours?"

"Johnny."

"Sooo…Johnny, how's school?"

"It's pretty lame," he replied with a slight shrug of one shoulder.

"Do you even know the definition of lame?"

He threw her a quick side-eye. "The opposite of cool?"

"What about your teachers?"

He looked back at the plane. "Lame."

"Let me guess…the girls there must be lame, too?"

A smirk titled his lips. "They're okay."

"Not the opposite of cool, eh?" she teased, nudging his arm. "What about friends? A totally *not* lame guy like you must have a few of those."

"I have enough," he said with another little smirk. He suddenly turned to face her, frowning. "Is that guy out there my real dad?"

Air whooshed from Bexley's lungs, making drawing in another breath impossible. "Why would you ask that?"

"I realized a couple of years ago that I must've been adopted. I don't look anything like Diego, and I once heard him arguing with my mom—he said something about my *real* mom."

Bexley's jaw worked as she held the boy's curious gaze, unable to articulate a safe reply. She let out a relieved breath at the sight of Jack boarding the aircraft. As he started for them, his expression was relaxed enough that she assumed his conversation with Tabitha had gone well.

"Hey, buddy," Jack greeted Johnny. "It's nice to finally meet you. My name is Jack Squires."

As he crouched in front of his son, Tabitha appeared in the aircraft's doorway, arms crossed and lips held in a rigid line. Bexley half expected lasers to shoot out of her ice-cold glare.

Johnny carefully scrutinized Jack's face. "If you're my real dad, can I come live with you?"

Jack's eyes darted over to Bexley.

"I didn't say *a word*," she promised with a shake of her head.

"I'm not stupid," Johnny said in a defiant tone.

Chuckling, Jack patted his son's knee. "I didn't figure you would be."

Johnny's voice cracked when he asked, "What took you so long to find me?"

To Jack's credit, he didn't turn around to throw blame on the evil woman standing behind him. Tears filled his eyes as he cleared his throat. "That's complicated, Johnny. Trust me, I wish someone would've told me about you the day you were born. I missed out on way too much." He gave his son a warm smile. "That's all going to change because from this point forward, we're going to spend as much time together as possible, getting to know each other. Is that alright with you?"

A tear rolled down Johnny's cheek when he nodded. "Can I call you 'Dad'?"

Jack choked out another chuckle when he pulled his son into his arms. "I'd be honored."

When Johnny's arms wrapped around his father's neck, Bexley felt the irritating prick of emotion stirring behind her eyes. She had to fill Brewer in on her suspicion that she was pregnant.

CHAPTER SIXTEEN

On Bexley's drive back to the office following the emotional introduction of Jack to his son, she couldn't stop thinking about her own pending situation. She couldn't put off telling Brewer any longer, or it would eat her up inside. She wasn't sure how he would react to the idea that he might be a father again after he'd lost his only other child to a horrific act of violence.

There was no doubt Brewer would be an excellent father. But she felt she'd be forcing him into the role since they had both decided not to have children. Maybe she could try one of those home tests before getting too worked up over the idea.

As she contemplated calling Brewer to see if he

could meet her for a late lunch, her dashboard screen lit with a call from her trusted assistant.

"What's up, Red?"

"I've been digging as deep as possible into this Arnold Douglas character's history, like you asked," Red began before pausing. "Bex…it isn't good."

Bexley gripped the steering wheel until her fingers were bloodless. "What did you find?"

"I couldn't locate any employment records after he was let go from a parts factory in the late seventies. It seems he lived off disability checks from the government. And the man moved around a lot after leaving Papaya Springs in the early eighties. Los Angeles, New York, Louisiana, Florida—he inhabited several big cities for quite some time before moving to the next one. He even spent a few months overseas in London, Rome, Paris, and several other major European cities."

A cold, crippling chill gripped Bexley's spine. Those were the same cities Twila had visited in her younger days. *He'd been tracking her.* "What did you find?"

"The dates he spent in each city coordinated around the same timeframes as a long list of women who went missing and were never found. We're talking at least a dozen women, maybe more. And over half of them were artists."

The air in Bexley's vehicle was both too stale and too thin. Her sweet neighbor had unknowingly become involved with one of the most dangerous men in history.

"We may be dealing with a serial killer," she choked out.

"Exactly what I was thinking, boss lady."

Bexley cracked her window with a shaking hand and gulped in the fresh ocean air. "Good work, Red. I'll contact Deputy Danks to fill him in on what you found and swing by Twila's to update the deputy keeping watch over her place. It's imperative everyone involved knows what we're dealing with."

"That includes you," Red warned in an ominous tone. "Be careful…watch your back."

After ending the call, Bexley didn't make it far before she was forced to pull into a gas station.

It seemed her period had arrived.

After grabbing the necessary supplies and cleaning up in the restroom, Bexley returned to her Explorer with a gas station burrito and a burst of determination to find Arnold Douglas before he hurt Twila. As she swiped through the dashboard screen to call the deputy, another call came in.

From J.J.

The second she accepted his call, J.J. began to speak.

"She's gone, darlin'," he gasped, desperate for air. "I was only in the restroom for a moment… bastard knocked me out cold when I re-entered the hallway. The deputy outside claims he'd been watching the property closely and didn't see anyone approach from the road. That murdering son-of-a-bitch has her, Bexley. He has her, and I don't know what to do about it."

Bexley inhaled sharply. If Twila's ex-lover hurt her, Bexley would never forgive herself for not finding him sooner.

"Hang tight, J.J. I'm on my way. We'll find her, I promise."

Angry tears stung her eyes as she punched the accelerator.

Brewer furiously paced behind Bexley and J.J. as the former coworkers hovered over Bexley's phone, carefully reviewing the security footage captured on the app. Once Bexley had called Brewer at his shop to fill him in on Twila's disappearance, her husband dropped everything to join them in the search. Bexley had secretly loved it when he showed up with grease smudged across one of his cheeks and along a forearm. Her husband was fiercely loyal to everyone he loved and didn't care about trivial things. He would've been too focused on Twila's safety to regard his reflection on the drive home.

Deputy Danks and a good portion of the Sheriff's Department were searching for any signs of Arnold Douglas or Twila. Bexley's pulse raced as she willed one of them to call, letting them know the alleged killer had been captured. Even if J.J. hadn't been knocked unconscious, Bexley knew Twila would never have merely snuck away for any reason. Twila cared deeply about J.J. and knew he was in a fragile condition the way it was. And as much as their neighbor openly adored Bexley and Brewer, Twila wouldn't dream of making them fear for her safety any more than they already had.

"I don't understand it," Brewer sulked, his voice exceptionally low and deep. "The cameras should've covered every angle."

"I'm sure you did everything right, Son," J.J. drawled in reply, holding a bag of frozen peas against the back of his head where he was knocked unconscious. Against Bexley's wishes, he had refused to allow her to call an ambulance to check on his injuries. "He's clearly not as smart as we are. We'll find something."

"If the officer didn't see anything from the front of the house, it has to mean our perp snuck in through a blind spot in back," Bexley told them. She switched to the backyard camera footage, replaying it in slow motion.

J.J. jabbed a finger at the phone's screen. "There! What was that? Back it up a little."

Bexley rewound the footage for several seconds. A hulking shadow the size of a large adult male flittered across the small screen, passing through Twila's backyard. Bexley rewound it a second time and paused the footage so they could examine the shadow in greater detail.

J.J.'s bushy brows drew together. "Is that a—"

"Cane," Bexley answered, meeting Brewer's enraged gaze.

"Bastard must've come in oceanside," J.J. snarled while gritting his teeth. "Would'a been easy to pretend he was just some civilian out on a casual stroll. I'm guessin' he broke in through the side window. Took 'er out that way, too."

Brewer nudged between them to get a closer look at Bexley's phone. "You're right. The way he stayed out of view, I'd bet he knew exactly where the cameras were installed." Venom dripped from his voice when he added, "He's probably been keeping an eye on the place ever since the night I thought I chased him away."

Rage clenched Bexley's entire body as she stared at the shadow. "Based on what Twila said, I'm surprised he had the strength to muscle his way inside, knock J.J. out, and drag Twila back through that window. Even though it was a lifetime ago he was injured, the fact that he's using a cane must mean he never fully recovered. And he's no spring chicken either."

Turning to Bexley, J.J.'s features took on a defeated expression. It was something she thought she'd never witness on her wise mentor. "What do you think he's gonna do with her?"

She swallowed past the lump in her throat and carefully assessed the situation. Under entirely different circumstances, she would have given him a hard time for not anticipating the perp's next move better than his mentee. "If he intended to hurt her, he most likely would've taken you both out here, on the spot, rather than going through the trouble of taking her somewhere else. Twila's smart, J.J. She'll figure out how to keep him calm and talk him out of whatever he may have planned." She nudged Brewer. "Have you been by the old rail yard lately?"

The way Brewer looked at her, she already knew his brain was on the same wavelength. "Let's see if that old apartment building is still standing."

"Stay here in case she returns," Bexley ordered J.J., grabbing the keys to Brewer's GTO and tossing them at her husband. "You drive. I'll call Danks on the way."

As soon as the old rail yard came into view, Bexley stiffened. Though most of the factories had been torn down ages ago, an ancient two-story brick building leaning to one side remained. Twila's description of the dilapidated apartment was spot-on.

"I can't believe it's still here," Bexley muttered.

"No cars in sight," Brewer observed as he pulled his classic car into the lot. "Maybe he took her somewhere else."

"Twila described him as being sentimental," Bexley reminded him with a slight shake of her head. "And she told us he never went out, never had any friends. I can't imagine any other place he would want to go."

Brewer locked his hand around her elbow when she reached for the passenger door handle. "Wait for Danks to get here."

"But—"

"We know Douglas has access to a gun," Brewer reminded her, his tone firm. "You're not going inside there empty-handed, B. And before you say it, this is *not* about me telling you what to do. I'm reminding you to use your head when I know damn well you're too busy listening to your heart."

She wrapped her arms beneath her chest as she held his stare. "This isn't just about my heart, Hawk. This guy is extremely dangerous."

"I'm scared for her, too," he said, sinking a hand into the nape of her hair behind her head and rubbing his fingers against her skull. "Still, we're not going to do her any good if we barge in there without a way to take him down."

"There's something I haven't told you…I didn't want to freak J.J. out. Red called right before Twila was kidnapped. She found evidence linking Arnold

Douglas to maybe a dozen missing women in the same cities Twila told us she had visited when she was younger." Tears stung the back of her eyes. "I don't think the woman he murdered in Papaya Springs was his first kill."

Brewer released her head to swipe a hand through his hair. "Shit."

"Exactly." Bexley tapped her phone screen to see if she had missed anything from Deputy Danks. She had worked directly with him as the sheriff never regarded her concerns with the authority they deserved. "If Danks doesn't get here soon—"

Two sounds simultaneously cut her off.

The unmistakable ring of a gunshot coming from the apartment building.

And a woman's scream.

CHAPTER SEVENTEEN

The moment Bexley heard the gunfire from within the apartment complex, she was on the run. She barely had time to register the sounds of Brewer swearing and slamming the driver's door before he was a few steps behind.

Bexley didn't pause as she entered the building. She used lighter steps and strained to listen for other sounds to give Twila's location away. She remembered Twila saying she wasn't sure how Arnie would make it upstairs alone with a bad leg, so she started up the broken stairway. It was a difficult feat as over half the wooden treads were either splintered out in spots or threatened to snap beneath her weight.

Once again, she was baffled as to how a man

with a debilitating injury could finesse his way up the broken stairway while holding a woman captive. Especially when she could hear Brewer hissing beneath his breath as he ascended the steps behind her. A few seconds in, a loud crack sounded from below, followed by the muffled *thud* of wood hitting the concrete floor beneath them.

Bexley braced herself, praying Arnold hadn't heard the noise. When no one came running, she whirled around to find her husband standing on the edge of a freshly broken step. Enough of them were missing then, making it impossible for him to finish the climb.

Brewer shook his head with a look of warning etched into his beautiful brown eyes. *"Please don't,"* he mouthed.

"I love you," she mouthed before clearing the final steps and heading down the hallway.

There was no need to press her ear against the only closed door as she could hear everything through the thin walls.

"Please, Arnie," Twila pleaded. "There's a better way to solve this. I understand I hurt you, and I can't say I'm sorry enough. There are trained professionals at the VA who can help—"

"I don't need help!" a low voice rumbled. "I only need you!"

"We were different people back then," Twila continued, her voice thick with tears. "I'm not the same girl you fell in love with. Holding me hostage and threatening to shoot us both isn't going to solve anything. It's time for you to move on."

"Move on?" the low voice sneered. "That's not an option! I've spent *decades* searching for you, my little mouse! In that time, other women were forced to suffer because you remained hidden!"

"What do you mean, 'they were forced to suffer'? Arnie, who were they? What did you do to them?"

"With every city I visited, every gallery I entered, and you weren't there, my bitterness grew. I had to release my anger somehow…I had to take it out on someone before I went completely insane."

"What did you do?" Twila whispered.

"I did what needed to be done."

"How many women did you hurt?"

"I didn't *hurt* them! I ended their pain of living in a hard and cruel world!"

Bexley stiffened with the raw emotion projected in Arnold's tone. If Twila didn't find a way to calm him down, the situation would escalate. She lowered to her stomach with as much care as possible, hoping the change in position didn't cause the floorboards to groan from her weight. Beneath the door, she could make out Twila's legs and only part of her capturer's. Twila was tied to a chair. Bexley couldn't tell whether or not Arnie still had the gun in his hands.

The way Twila's gasp was stifled, Bexley imagined the woman doing it behind a hand held over her lips. "You mean…you killed them?"

"Don't worry, little mouse. They were respectfully laid to rest in the backyard of whatever home I inhabited at the time."

"You must realize I could never be with someone who murdered innocent women," Twila told him in a tone that was still gentle despite the resolution of her words. "You need to turn yourself in, Arnie. Those women deserve justice."

Arnie released a strained chuckle. "You expect me to *willingly* choose to rot in jail now that I've found you?"

"I expect you to do the right thing. The soldier I met at the bus station was a good man. Surely he's still in there…somewhere."

"You never thought I was good enough for you."

"Of course I did!"

"Not with this bum leg. That's why you left, isn't it? That's why you wouldn't marry me when I asked."

"It had nothing to do with you or your leg, you old fool. You seem perfectly healed now. Why do you still carry a cane around when you clearly don't need it?"

Bexley watched as a set of legs in a worn pair of khakis shuffled closer to Twila. "While we're on the subject of 'old fools,'" Arnold sneered, "who was that geezer with the earring lurking in your house?"

"J.J. is a noble man…one who spent many years executing justice because it's the right thing to do."

"Are you saying you'll settle down with that hippie?" Arnold asked, his voice thick with amusement. "After all these years of being a 'free soul' or whatever the hell you claimed to be, you will finally decide to become domesticated?"

"I said no such thing."

When the man stalked the remaining distance to Twila and bent right in front of her, the silver glint of a pistol caught Bexley's eye. *Find a reason for him to set it down,* she willed Twila.

"Then what are you saying?" he snarled.

Bexley held her breath and adjusted her position, hoping for a better vantage point.

Twila inhaled sharply.

Bexley's pulse pounded against her temples as she held her breath. Was he holding the gun to Twila's head?

Had Twila seen Bexley's shadow move beneath the door?

"This conversation is going nowhere," Twila informed him. "At least not until you set that deadly weapon down so we can act like civilized adults. Really, Arnold. You claimed you know me better than anyone. If that's true, prove it. Stop using unnecessary force to make me answer your questions, and talk to me like a real man. Set that ridiculous thing on the table and look me in the eye while you speak."

Bexley briefly closed her eyes. *Atta girl, Twila.*

For a moment, the legs clad in khaki twill didn't move.

Then, mercifully, they shuffled away from Twila, and the sound of heavy metal meeting wood broke the silence.

Bexley quietly moved to her feet and tried the door handle. It was unlocked.

"There!" Arnold barked. "You happy now?"

In the next rapid heartbeat, Bexley turned the handle the rest of the way and barged inside. Arnold whirled around with a bewildered look. Bexley faltered, taken aback by the size of the man standing before her. He was far from weak and feeble for an elderly man. He was in excellent shape. *Probably so he could overpower his victims,* Bexley thought with a disgusted sneer.

When the wail of multiple sirens pierced the air, Arnold hesitated.

Bexley sprang forward.

"No, Bexley!" Twila pleaded a moment too late.

Bexley struck his neck with the palm of her hand, moving so quickly that he didn't have time to react before she kneed him in the groin. She then lunged at the pistol, securing it only seconds before Arnold recovered and moved toward her.

"Stop right there," Bexley warned, releasing the safety and pointing the barrel at him. "Don't move a muscle, or I'll shoot." As much as she loathed guns, she'd been trained to properly handle them and would discharge the weapon if it would save her life and Twila's.

She must've hesitated enough to reveal her aversion to the pistol because Arnold charged at her anyway.

The pistol was knocked from her hand and slid across the floor beneath Twila.

Arnold lunged again, using his entire body as a weapon. Twila screamed behind them as Bexley and Arnold landed in the hallway with Arnold on top. Fortunately, Brewer had spent countless hours teaching Bexley ways to defend herself without a weapon. Before giving Arnold another second to think, she violently twisted her hips to one side, knocking him over and spinning him around to his back so she was on top.

His hands wrapped around her neck and began to squeeze. Bexley sputtered beneath the press of his thumbs.

"Arnie, stop!" Twila cried. "Don't you dare hurt her!"

The old man was strong. Lucky for Bexley, he also seemed to underestimate the abilities of a woman her size. She lifted her shoulders and dropped her chin, shrinking the girth of his hold. She cupped one of his arms and reached back to pry his middle finger away from her shoulder until she felt it snap. The move elicited a howl of pain from Arnold, allowing her a chance to move away from him as he tended to his wounded digit.

As she started back toward the pistol and Twila,

a meaty hand wrapped around her ankle, sweeping her feet out beneath her and knocking her to the floor. With his wounded finger tucked against his chest, Arnold pulled himself up to stand, presumably to stomp on her. She recovered and started to spring to her feet.

But she was two seconds too late.

Arnold slammed into her at running speed before she could regain footing, propelling them into the air.

The battered apartment building whirled around Bexley with the violence of a cheap carnival ride as she soared over the stairway and tumbled over the last few steps.

Upon landing, she was sure her body was shattered into pieces. It definitely felt like it. She was utterly immobilized with pain.

Fortunately, her buttocks and torso had taken the brunt of the fall, seemingly leaving her skull unharmed. With the sound of a deep, wet cough, she turned her head to see the murderer sputtering blood from his lips.

A large chunk of a broken stair tread protruded from his chest.

Their eyes met as he shuddered with his last breath.

White-hot pain crackled through her chest when she tried to let out a relieved breath.

It was over.

Arnold Douglas would never hurt another woman.

"Don't move, Bexley," she heard Deputy Danks say from nearby. "The EMTs are right outside. They'll be here any second."

Brewer was suddenly kneeling at her side. Even though the outline of his face was nothing more than a blur, she recognized his masculine scent and the familiar weight of his unyielding presence. "I love you, my beautiful, frustratingly stubborn wife." His voice was calm. Steady. "You're going to be okay…I promise."

His fingers wrapping around hers were the last thing her brain registered before shutting down.

CHAPTER EIGHTEEN

The mechanical whirl and beep of machines filled Bexley's ears as she slowly regained consciousness. Her eyes flipped open to find a slender blonde with thick French braids in colorful scrubs hovering above her reclined body.

The woman—presumably a nurse, considering Bexley was definitely in a hospital bed—smiled warmly. She was young and annoyingly chipper. "Welcome back, Mrs. Hawkins."

Bexley's throat was too dry to form an audible response. Sensing her discomfort, the nurse handed over a glass of water containing a bendy straw. When Bexley bent upright to take a drink, excruciating pain gripped her chest like a vice. She also noticed her right arm was in a sling.

"You'll have to take it easy for a while," the nurse told her. "You sprained your wrist, broke a few ribs, and sustained a considerable amount of internal bruising." Sympathy radiated from her expression as she touched Bexley's shoulder. "You suffered some other injuries as well. I'll leave those for the doctor to explain. She's finishing up with another patient and should be here soon."

Nodding slightly, Bexley brought the straw to her lips and sucked down the room-temperature liquid. After handing the glass back to the nurse, Bexley slowly lowered back down through gritted teeth. She closed her eyes, willing the throbbing pain in her ribs to subside. "My husband, Brewer... Twila..."

"They're both camped out in the waiting room along with half a dozen others your husband introduced as your friends and family. Your husband hasn't left since you were first brought in. After the doctor speaks with you, I can send him back if you'd like."

Bexley gave her a minuscule nod. "Please."

The "others" would include her sister, Temperance, and Kiersten, but she didn't have the energy to talk to them. At least not yet.

"How's your pain?" the nurse asked. "What would you give it on a scale of one to ten?"

With a sharp pain pressing against her side, Bexley hissed through her teeth. "Are we talking the *Richter* scale? Because it feels like I was sucked into the earth's atmosphere and spit back out."

"I'll give you a little extra bump," the nurse offered with a hint of amusement.

"You're an angel."

When Bexley opened her eyes again, a brunette 50-something woman in a white coat with bright green eyes and a no-nonsense haircut beamed down on her.

Bexley wasn't sure if she had drifted asleep or if the doctor entered the room mere seconds after the nurse left. Either way, she suspected the drip attached to her hand was supplying her with a liquid painkiller because she was starting to feel a little floaty.

"I'm Dr. Becker. It's an honor to meet the heroic investigator responsible for cleaning house in Papaya Springs. I only wish we were meeting under more pleasant circumstances."

"Let's not be dramatic, Doc," Bexley rasped. "What's the verdict?"

"You took quite the beating. Luckily, none of

your injuries were either life-threatening or required surgery. After one of the sheriff's deputies showed me pictures of the crime scene, I'd say it's nothing short of a miracle your skull is still fully intact. However, you broke several ribs, and I suspect you bruised some as well. There could be bruising to other vital organs. I'd like to order an MRI to ensure we aren't missing anything vital."

The doctor paused and crossed her arms with a thoughtful expression. "Mrs. Hawkins—"

"Please, call me Bexley."

"Bexley, when did you last have a menstrual period?"

A sob lodged inside Bexley's throat as she met the woman's knowing gaze. "I'm not sure. Six or eight weeks? I suspected I was pregnant…until I started spotting earlier today."

"This was before you fell?"

With tears blurring her vision, Bexley dipped her chin slowly. "It was maybe an hour or two before that."

"I suspect you may have suffered a miscarriage. I'd like to take another blood test in forty-eight hours to confirm."

"I understand." Bexley blinked the tears away. She hadn't been expecting that. Even though she hadn't planned for a child, it still broke her heart to think of the life that she had lost.

Brewer appeared in the doorway with a large bouquet of bright flowers. The heat of his loving gaze burned a hole through Bexley, sticking to her insides like napalm.

"There's my girl," he rasped with the kind of glowing smile that had a way of curing anything that ailed Bexley—except for that time. Her ribs throbbed when she threw him a tiny wave. His eyes shifted to the doctor. "Should I come back?"

"No, Mr. Hawkins, we're basically finished here. I'd like to run a few more tests over the next couple of days to rule out any other issues I may have missed before she's released. But at this point, as long as your wife takes it easy for the next six to eight weeks, she should heal nicely and be as good as new." The doctor patted Bexley's shoulder before she backed away. "She's all yours."

Brewer grinned at the woman as she passed him on her way out. "Thanks, Doc."

Tucking a well of emotions away as deeply as she could muster, Bexley held out her hand stuck with the IV for Brewer to take. "Hey, handsome."

His fingers wrapped around hers. "How do you feel?"

"Kinda like a serial killer threw me down a broken stairway."

He sucked on his lips for a moment, holding her gaze with an intensity that made her shiver. "I'm not going to lecture you because I would've done the same damn thing if I had been in your shoes and not too damn heavy to scale those steps. You're no damsel, B. I get it. I just wish you understood how much you mean to me. If you hadn't survived that fall—"

"We need to talk," she blurted.

"Not necessary." His voice cracked a little as he continued. "The doctor told me everything while you were still passed out." His fingers caressed the back of her hand. "Are you doing okay?"

Wordlessly, she gave him a hesitant nod and a half-hearted smile. She didn't trust herself to say anything without breaking down, and she suspected the pain in her ribs would become unbearable.

Moisture in Brewer's eyes shined beneath the neon lights when he set the bouquet on the table beside the bed. He tucked his free hand inside his jeans pocket, all at once looking like a lost little boy when he asked, "Is it alright if I kiss you?"

She released a sound that could have qualified

as a laugh or a sob. "I might break another rib crying if you don't."

He removed his hand from his pocket and threaded it inside her hair as their lips met. For a blissful handful of moments, her strength was fully restored with the reminder of his fierce love. His lips caressed hers with the same mix of emotions knotting inside her gut. They had been through countless tragedies since they first met, and their bond was stronger than ever.

They would survive this, too.

Brewer left Bexley's side long enough to give Twila and J.J. a turn. Their short time with her was emotionally draining as Twila was full of tears and apologies that Bexley refused to accept. Even J.J. shed a few tears, which was overwhelming in itself.

Several hours later, after Brewer had gone home to check on Cap and Bexley had escaped the pain with another comfortable nap, a hesitant knock came from the doorway.

It was somewhat jarring to see Deputy Danks wearing jean shorts and a well-worn band t-shirt with flip-flops. Bexley had worked with him on so many cases that she sometimes forgot he'd been a potential up-and-coming actor before they'd met with looks good enough to have launched him into stardom. If it weren't for the way his dark hair was shorn down on the sides to military length, he could be mistaken as a PSC student strolling through campus.

"Up for some company?" Deputy Danks asked, his chin held low as he smiled.

"For Papaya Springs's future star detective?" Bexley winked. "Always."

"Let's not get ahead of ourselves. After all, you did the heavy lifting on this case." He shuffled inside and stopped alongside her bed to gently squeeze her shoulder. "Glad to see you alive and looking well, Bexley."

She clicked her tongue. "My makeup artist called in sick today. I must look atrocious."

Danks released a boyish grin. "You should see the other guy."

"I did," Bexley seethed through clenched teeth. "I had the pleasure of watching the bastard take his last breath."

The deputy nodded gravely. "Douglas was pronounced dead on the scene. We already got a statement from Twila. When you're feeling up to it, we'd also like to take your statement."

"Did she tell you the details of his other murders?"

"She did. I consulted with the FBI, and they'll take it from here. They're arranging to excavate the backyard of every home Douglas lived in between now and nineteen seventy-six. Hopefully, they can provide answers for the family members of those missing girls and give them peace."

Bexley caught herself before she let out a deep sigh. Although the pain was considerably less, some things still caused unnecessary pain. "Do you ever wonder if you made a mistake by choosing to become an officer of the law? Just think, you could be rubbing shoulders with Hollywood's elite by now, sucking champagne off each other's backends and snorting caviar, or whatever it is movie stars do with their free time."

"I think they *eat* caviar," he said with a quiet laugh. "But nah, that scene isn't for me."

"Sometimes I worry I'm going to give Hawk an honest-to-god heart attack. What does your girl-friend think about you chasing after killers?"

"Hawk is a resilient guy…I shouldn't have to remind you of that. And Angie doesn't have to worry about it anymore." The deputy paused to rub his forehead. "I've been officially relieved of my duties. Sheriff Blair was upset that I'd been contacting you directly. He doesn't think I'm a good team player."

"He *fired you*?" she spat, jerking upright in a way that set her chest on fire. "You're the best deputy he has! That dirty, low-life, bottom-feeding—"

"It's okay," Danks interjected with a crooked grin, motioning for her to calm down. "I hated working for him anyway."

"What are you going to do now?"

He lifted one shoulder. "I don't know…maybe go to college and get a degree in criminal justice. Maybe I'll decide to become a lawyer or something instead. Money will be tight for a while because rent isn't exactly cheap, but I think I could get a scholarship—"

"Come work for me!" Bexley blurted. "Technically, you'd work under J.J. since I have a handful of months left before I can apply for my P.I. license. But as owner of Stronghold Investigations, I have the authority to hire you!"

His green eyes widened. "Really?"

"Adam, you shouldn't act so surprised! You're whip-smart and as determined to work as a jackrabbit. I'd be honored to have you on my team! Besides, I'll need someone to handle my files in the time the doctor said it'll take me to recover from this. You can take on as much or as little as you want. I can still advise you while I'm out. It'd be the perfect arrangement for both of us!"

He gave her a hesitant look. "You seem *really* stoked about this. Like, unnaturally so. How doped up are you right now?"

"Pretty doped," she replied with a wink. "But the doctor said my brain's good to go, and it's telling me this is a brilliant idea. Go home and think about it. You can ask me again as soon as I'm free of whatever narcotics they're pumping into me."

"I might just take you up on that." He tipped an imaginary hat with a smile that lit his entire face. "Thanks a million. Take care of yourself, Squires."

"You too, Hollywood."

CHAPTER NINETEEN

A month and a half after the showdown with Arnold Douglas, Bexley woke from a nap, her body aching considerably less with every movement. Her eyes focused on a set of monstrous suitcases with matching duffel bags outside the bedroom door. They weren't anything she recognized, and the high-end aluminum designs weren't her husband's style.

"Hawk?" she called out, scooting into an upright position. When the toilet flushed in the attached bathroom, she added, "If you're sick of taking care of me, I get it. But whatever baroness you think you're running off with will have to go through me first, and I think I've proven that I can be a hard woman to take down."

Brewer emerged from the bathroom with a towel slung low on his hips, moisture from his wet hair dripping down his sculpted chest. "What are you babbling on about, Squires?"

She flung a hand at the doorway. "Those ridiculous suitcases! I've done a decent job of taming the bad boy in you, but come on. You're no Kardashian."

"You and me are goin' on a trip." His dimples popped into place with a wide grin, and his eyebrows wagged before he bent to kiss her. *God help me*, she thought as their lips melded together. *One of these times, my heart will literally explode.*

Once he withdrew from her, she smiled at him with the finesse of a smitten schoolgirl. "With that godawful luggage?"

He eyed the suitcases and chuckled before plopping down on the mattress at her side. "Take that up with your two best friends and sister. I don't even know what's *inside*. They won't give us the combination until we arrive at our destination. Kiersten assured me they've supplied us with everything we will need."

As Bexley pictured Kiersten, Temperance, and Cineste shopping together on her behalf, she rolled her eyes and groaned. While the women collectively possessed excellent taste, they tended to go overboard. "*Where* are we going?"

"On the honeymoon I promised but never gave you."

A warm flutter rippled through her chest. The man couldn't be any more romantic. "But *where*?"

"It's a surprise." Lacing his hands behind his head, his eyes didn't leave hers as he lowered to his back. Then sat upright. Then lowered again.

"Have mercy," she muttered. Her beautiful husband was doing sit-ups right before her hungry eyes. If she weren't in so much pain from her tussle with Twila's ex-lover, she would've attacked her husband at that moment.

"You say something?" he asked, quirking an eyebrow during another sit-up.

"Quit distracting me with that godawful body of yours. Seriously, Hawk. I'm gonna go blind. Such an *atrocity*."

With a snigger, he kept going. "You might want to get ready, B. We have company coming."

"I'm failing to follow you here. If we're leaving, why are people coming?"

"You'll find out."

She tossed her hands out at her sides. "I can't just up and leave, Brewer. I have clients—open cases that need my attention. I've been out for almost an entire week already."

"Danks has everything under control," he answered. "After everything you've been through, you've earned a real vacation. The doc even said it would be beneficial if you took some extra time off." He finally paused his workout to frame her face inside one of his hands and run his thumb along her jaw. "We've had an emotional couple of months, B. A little extra time alone together, extra space to heal our souls would do us both good."

There was no sense in arguing any longer. He was absolutely right.

They met in the middle for a drawn-out kiss filled with endless emotions. Brewer cradled her in the most gentle of holds, knowing she still hurt. He eventually ended the kiss and regarded her with a grin. "I wasn't kidding about company coming. They'll be here in half an hour."

Grunting under her breath, she rolled out of bed and shuffled into their bathroom to start the shower.

"Kiersten said you're supposed to wear the outfit in the garment bag hanging on your side," Brewer called out. "And you're supposed to wear those gold sandals she bought you in Greece."

"Everyone in my life is so bossy," she mumbled as she stepped under the warm spray. The heat on her sore muscles felt heavenly. She would've been tempted to stand under it longer if she hadn't heard Brewer shout that she only had twenty minutes left.

Shuffling into the closet, she unzipped the bag from Kiersten's favorite department store and gasped. The most beautiful dress she'd ever seen hung from a velvet hanger. The chiffon material, with its A-line cut and v-neck with cap sleeves, was the perfect level of femininity without being too revealing. The pleated material around the waist gave it a touch of class. And it was pure white.

Bexley covered her mouth. "Is this—"

"We can't leave on a honeymoon without a proper wedding reception," Brewer answered from right behind her.

She spun on her bare heels to see her husband dressed in a loose, white linen button-down and off-white khaki trousers. Although it was more casual than the navy suit he had worn when they eloped on the beach, the casual look was more enduring on her husband. If Brad Pitt himself were standing at her husband's side, Bexley wouldn't have been more starstruck by handsomeness.

With an overwhelming rush of affection for the

beautiful man who had transformed her mediocre life into her own fairytale, Bexley threw herself into his arms and swallowed the tears rising in her throat. "I love you, Brewer Hawkins. Now and always."

As fireworks shot over their heads, launched by Danks from a temporary station nearby in the sand, Bexley and Brewer kissed passionately in front of their closest friends and family. Cheers erupted before they were pulled into an endless string of embraces and well-wishes. Cap and Cinderella yipped happily alongside the partygoers before chasing each other up and down the beach.

Tabitha had allowed Johnny to attend the celebration with Jack, and the kid quickly become inseparable from Olive. It was good that the two children were well-occupied because Bexley caught Temperance and Jack kissing several times throughout the night. On one occasion, Jack caught Bexley's gaze on them, and she winked to let him know it was cool with her. Nothing could've ruined her joy that night.

As they prepared to leave for the trip—destination still unknown to Bexley—they gave tearful goodbyes to everyone in attendance. The suitcases filled with new wardrobes and God knew what else had been a group present from all of them, so Bexley and Brewer made a point to thank each of them for their generosity.

"We will take good care of your Captain," Temperance assured Bexley once she was huddled in a circle with her sister and best friends. "You have nothing to worry about."

"I have everything to worry about!" Bexley corrected her. "I don't know where my husband is taking me! Do I need special shots? Are we going on a flight? How long is it?"

"For once in your life, you'll have to sit back and relax, sis," Cineste said. "Trust that those who love you have handled every possible detail."

"Except for the malaria vaccine," Kiersten butted in. "You got that, right?"

Bexley's eyes popped wide. "*What?*"

"She's kidding," Cineste promised, giving their friend a playful shove. "Seriously though, Bex, you have to take a ton of pictures. We're all so jealous of your trip!"

"Great!" Bexley feigned their level of excitement. "Now someone tell me where I'm going!"

The women giggled, each taking a turn to hug Bexley before they walked away. Jack approached her next with a sheepish grin and hands in his pockets.

"This was some celebration," he said, turning to watch over his shoulder as Johnny and Olive each threw balls down the beach for the dogs. "I suppose I should get him to bed soon, or Carla might not approve another overnight visit."

Dipping her chin, Bexley smiled. "I'm glad she came to her senses. Does Johnny know about Tabitha yet?"

"Carla told him shortly after he met me. Johnny told her he'll always think of Tabitha as his aunt and Carla as his mom. The women seemed pretty satisfied with the arrangement. Tabitha's pleased she can go on with her life, status quo, and Carla seems grateful to have a little alone time without losing 'her son'."

Bexley laughed as Olive began chasing Johnny. "He seems like a great kid. Smart, too. Must be that Squires blood."

Jack's features sobered as his gaze locked with hers. "I don't know how to thank you for helping me, Bex. If I hadn't asked for your involvement, I may never have known I had a child."

"I'm sure you would've found your way to each other eventually. I'm glad I could help speed up the process." She tipped her chin in Temperance's connection. "Things seem to be going well between you and Temp."

Jack licked his lips and glanced down at his bare feet wedged in the sand. "I know I told you I'd take it slow with her, but we have this connection…it's pretty hard to fight it."

Brewer caught her gaze from where he stood in a huddle with Luke, Alex, and a couple of guys from his old motorcycle club. When he grinned, she grinned back, and her cheeks flushed. "It's okay, Jack. I know the feeling." She playfully slugged his shoulder. "Just don't hurt her."

"I won't." He leaned down to kiss her forehead. "Have fun on your honeymoon, Bex. Relax and let that husband spoil you the way you deserve. The four of us can meet up for dinner after you return."

Red was the next one to give the couple of honor her parting well-wishes, followed by Danks and his girlfriend.

The goodbye Bexley and Brewer saved for last was the hardest. Brewer put his arm around Bexley as they approached J.J. and Twila cuddled on the couch behind their house.

"You look good, Twila," Bexley said to her.

"And you're glowing, kiddo," was Twila's cheeky reply as she stood to embrace Bexley. "What you did was reckless and dangerous, but I wouldn't be here if you hadn't come to my rescue. For that, I thank you from the bottom of my heart. I've nearly completed a painting for you and your beautiful husband to show my gratitude. I hope to have it done by the time you return."

"That's not necessary. I'm just grateful you made it out of there alive."

"That makes two of us," J.J. wheezed, budging in to hug Bexley when Twila moved on to Brewer. Bexley couldn't recall ever receiving an embrace from her father anywhere near the caliber of the one J.J. gave. He even kissed the top of her head before whispering, "I owe you everything I've got."

"Inheriting your business was more than enough," she assured him with a gentle pat on his back before they released each other.

Brewer tucked Bexley against his side and nodded to the elderly couple. "Take care of each other while we're gone."

"We will," J.J. promised, slinging an arm around Twila's neck. "Make sure your wife stays out of trouble while you're gone. She rightfully earned a fair chunk of time away from this nefarious community."

Brewer's face split with a wide grin. "That should be easy enough, considering our destination."

The newlyweds headed to the front of the cottage and drove off in Brewer's GTO with their friends and family waving goodbye among shouts of good intentions. Someone had written "Just Married" on the back window, and a string of tin cans rattled from a string tied to the bumper. Bexley waved at their guests until they were no longer in sight, then wrapped herself around her husband's arm and released a heavy yawn.

"It's so late, darling husband. Are we seriously flying out tonight?"

"Temperance helped me time it just right. We'll sleep on the flight over—her jet has a queen-sized bed. By the time we wake, we should be there."

Bexley couldn't begin to imagine what Temperance had concocted, considering their wealthy friend had been offering to send them somewhere amazing on her private jet for years. "And where is *there*, again?"

He glanced down at her, eyebrows lifted. "Somewhere warm and secluded where no one will bother us unless we ring for service. You'll get the idea if you imagine feasting on a floating tray of fresh fruits and fancy chocolates while swimming beside one of those bungalows in the middle of nowhere."

With visions of a grass hut suspended over turquoise blue water, Bexley snuggled against her husband's shoulder and closed her eyes with a content sigh. Maybe having a rich and famous friend who insisted on showering them with decadent experiences wasn't so bad.

She couldn't deny that J.J. and Brewer were right—she *had* earned time away from Papaya Springs. She only hoped it was still standing by the time they returned.

While writing this book, I did not take the subject of miscarriage lightly. I edited and revised several scenes, even consulted with an OBGYN on the accuracy. I hope I presented it in a way that's sensitive to anyone who has suffered a similar situation. My heart goes out to every parent who has ever been in Bexley and Brewer's situation.

🩶Quinn

Thank you for reading *The Neighbor's Dark Past*! If you enjoyed this book, please take a quick minute to leave a review on Amazon, Goodreads, and

BookBub. Anything you can do to spread the word about this book is greatly appreciated!

Want to receive free bonus content, sneak peeks of upcoming releases, and access to my exclusive monthly giveaways? You'll also receive a FREE copy of my standalone, *What They Never Said*, when you sign up for my mailing list: www.quinnavery.com/subscribe

With over 40 captivating titles spanning various genres, Quinn Avery honed her talent for crafting intricate puzzles through her smart and quirky Bexley Squires mystery series. Her contemporary suspense thrillers, often set in her beloved locales such as Lake Shetek and Mankato, Minnesota, are nothing short of addictive, leaving readers spellbound with their mind-spinning twists.

For more information, and a free ebook, visit www.QuinnAvery.com.

ACKNOWLEDGMENTS

To my loyal Bexley fans: this one was for you! Man, I forgot how much I adore our spunky heroine and her crew. This book was a blast to write…so much that I'm certain there will be a #7 coming!

A big thank you to Najla Qamber and her team for knocking this cover out so quickly. I'm grateful to have your amazing talents at my disposal!

Thanks yet again to my bestie Christy Freeberg for reading the first draft and loving it (sorry but I love that you cried)!

Thank you to each and every reader who either purchased or rented this book. I would really appreciate it if you could please take a quick minute to leave a review (no matter how brief) on Amazon/Goodreads/BookBub!

Special thanks to my husband for putting up with me and continuing to support my crazy ideas! You're the best! 🤍